# Unshakable Love

# Other Works by Heather Justesen

# Unshakable Love

Book One in the Shelter Sisters Series

# HEATHER TULLIS

Published by Jelly Bean Press,
PO Box 548, Osawatomie, KS 66064
ISBN: 978-1-63034-081-0

Cover design by Heather Justesen
Cover design © 2019 by Heather Justesen
Cover art Adobe Stock Photos #140859214 by Paul

# Dedication

For Pauline—
whose support makes all of this easier.

# One

MEENA DIDN'T EVER WANT to stand up again.

She had just gotten off a double-shift at the plastics plant across town and returned home to the tiny apartment she shared with her roommate, Bennett, and their two kids. She stretched out on the lumpy sofa in the suffocating July heat to rest for a few minutes—her evening routine would still be there when her feet stopped throbbing.

If she was lucky, her almost three-year-old son, Deven would sleep for a few hours before he woke needing a bathroom break. Meena didn't know what she would do if it weren't for Bennett. When the two of them had decided to pool their resources at the women's shelter so they could get out and afford an apartment, she hadn't expected them to still be rooming together over two years later, but the arrangement had worked and she hadn't been able to secure a better paying job in the jewelry industry again. Hopefully her side job of making and selling items on Etsy would eventually take off.

She could always dream.

When she had broken ties with her disapproving Indian parents to marry a nice, white Catholic Army paratrooper nearly five years ago, she hadn't imagined she would end up in this position: a widowed single mom, broke, and working scut to make ends meet. Barely.

Seven hours until she headed back in for the early shift. She should be in bed. But first she needed just a few more minutes of peace and quiet.

A fist pounded on the thin door to the hallway. "Meena, Bennett, open up."

It was Sheila, a third graduate from the shelter, who lived down the hall.

"Just a minute." Meena pitched her voice to hopefully reach the hall without waking up the kids. But maybe that was wishful thinking. She dragged herself off the lumpy sofa and opened the door two steps away.

"Neither of you are checking your phones, are you?" Sheila asked as she brought in a waft of the hallway's hot, stale air tinged with cigarette smoke into the apartment with her. She closed the door behind her, flipping the lock closed again. Despite the late hour, she still wore khaki shorts and a green t-shirt, and her light auburn hair was up in its usual ponytail.

"I think Bennett's asleep already. I just got off work and haven't turned my phone back on."

"Now you're going to wish you had." Sheila opened the door to the bedroom Bennett shared with her nine-year-old daughter, Grace. "Bennett," she said in a loud stage whisper.

"What?" Bennett muttered grumpily, her eyes still closed.

"Get in here." Sheila's voice brooked no denials.

Bennett sighed deeply and dragged herself off the bed, half stumbling into the living room and closing the door behind her. She ran a hand through her blond curls and glared. "I just got to sleep. This better be good."

"It's better than good. It's amazing. Seriously," Sheila grabbed the baby monitor and Meena's apartment key that were both sitting on the kitchen counter and pulled them down the hall to her apartment, barely pausing to lock the door behind them.

"What is it? I need to go to bed," Meena complained, though she was curious—Sheila wasn't usually so insistent.

"You won't be tired when you hear this."

Meena could hear excited female voices before they even opened the door. Andrea—Sheila's roommate—as well as Vanna, and Dierdre, who had apartments on the floor above—all of them friends and former residents from the shelter—were seated in the living room.

"Can you believe it?" Vanna asked, jumping to her feet. She must have met with a client that day because she still wore one of the skirt and blouse combos she favored for business.

"Believe what? Sheila didn't tell us anything," Bennett grumbled.

"We won," Andrea said, pumping a fist toward the ceiling, and tossing back her tight African American curls in jubilation.

"What?" It took Meena a moment to spot the lotto ticket lying on the refurbished coffee table in front of them. Wait. It was Saturday night. She turned to Sheila. "Hold on, the ticket was actually worth something? What was it? A thousand dollars?" Oh, the jewelry supplies she could buy with even a sixth of that. Or she could be responsible and use it to get a tune up for her car...

Andrea was the one who answered. "No, honey, we won the jackpot. Seventeen. Million. Dollars."

Meena just stared at Andrea, trying to make her brain compute.

4

Bennett on the other hand, screamed in excitement and jumped around the room, suddenly as alert as Sheila had promised before. "No way, really? No way! That's insane. Are you sure?"

"Sure as we can be. Of course, we have to turn in the ticket and hope someone else didn't have the same numbers to split the winnings—it's already being split six ways," Sheila said.

"Right, because how could we possibly survive on only eight and a half million," Vanna teased in her soft southern drawl.

It was starting to sink in. "Wait, seriously? We won? The jackpot?" Praise be to Ganesh.

"We sure did." Dierdre slung an arm around her shoulder.

Meena realized she would be able to quit her job at the plastics factory. Now *that* was something to celebrate.

Thankfully, Meena decided to wait until the money arrived before giving her notice at work, because the lotto commission did not move quickly and the women soon realized it would take months before they received any kind of payment. It only took a few weeks of being the new poster children for the American Lotto for them to decide they wanted to live near each other so their kids would grow up close and they could still help one another as needed.

Sheila had started collecting information about housing possibilities and they gathered together one evening in early August to discuss their options.

"I really liked that neighborhood," Andrea said, pointing to one Sheila had flagged on the map.

"But they don't have enough houses for sale," Dierdre said. "Besides, security would be a nightmare."

'What about that one?" Bennett suggested, pointing to a gated community on the west side of town.

"The homes are ridiculously expensive and the Covenants, Conditions, and Restrictions the HOA wrote are insane," Meena reminded.

"Besides, they're total snobs," Sheila said. "When I told them who we were and gave them my address to this building they literally wrinkled their noses in disgust."

"What if we just bought a piece of property and built six houses on it, made our own gated community?" Vanna suggested.

"That would mean either staying in this dump for at least a year—seriously, at least—or moving somewhere else and then moving again, and securing two separate locations," Dierdre objected. Of the six of them, she was the most concerned about security—and she knew more about it than the rest of them combined. The red-head was also the only one of them with a concealed-carry permit.

They had been sitting around Vanna's living room while the kids played in the other room for nearly an hour. The interruptions from kids were getting more frequent and it seemed like they weren't getting any closer to a solution. Meena rubbed the back of her neck and thought longingly of a long soak in a hot bath—which she couldn't take since they only had a shower stall. A tub was on her definite must-have list when they finally figured this out.

"There was one other option I looked into," Sheila said.

"What is it?" Meena asked.

Sheila tossed a black and white printout of the old six-story apartment building next to the community garden. "It has plenty of space for all of us, it would be considerably easier to monitor and secure. It's been on the market for a few years with no takers, so the owner would probably come down a bit into a reasonable range. It's across the street from the elementary school. And there would be options of either first, each of us taking a floor—which would be an insane amount of space—or two, splitting the top three floors in half and renovating and renting or selling the lower floors as condos or offices." She pulled some images from a folder, setting them out to show the current floor plan. "I had Charlee look it over and at a first glance she thought it was rehab-able, though she recommended a full demo down to the brick walls. It's way too big of a project for her new company, but she said she could hook us up with some larger, reputable companies to do the work."

"That's got to take a year or more as well," Bennett said with a sigh.

"Not if we do some quick basic upgrades, then moved into the second floor while the upper floors were being renovated. I know it's not ideal, but it's workable. And if we sold out the second and third floors as condos once we were settled upstairs, that would put money back in the coffers to manage upkeep and utilities for our floors."

"I did want storefront space. We could do that if we bought the building," Dierdre said. "But how do we secure a building if random people move into the other two floors?"

"Separate entrances?" Bennett suggested. "Maybe theirs only goes to their floors and ours only goes to our floors?"

"That would be doable," Dierdre nodded.

"We would need an inspection and estimates for the work, but it sounds interesting," Meena said.

"All in favor of looking into this more?" Vanna asked.

A loud chorus of ayes filled the room.

"I'll contact the Realtor for more information tomorrow," Sheila said.

Meena was glad they had an option they were all interested in at least. Maybe they could be settled there by Halloween. She could always dream.

# Two

WHO KNEW BECOMING a millionaire would be such a pain? Meena slid on her sunglasses and ball cap, feeling like one of those TV stars that had to disguise themselves to get a little privacy when they went out to get a burger. She had known when she stood for photographs with the other winners that her life was about to change. She hadn't realized that along with the freedom to pursue her passions instead of working a drudge job, she would also feel like she was living in a fish bowl.

It had been five months and she still got questions from people at the store, phone calls and letters from people asking for donations, and the occasional reporter trying to reach her for an interview. Also, she had to look over her shoulder every time she went outside, wondering if someone was going to pop out from around a corner, thanks to the strange emails she had been getting for the past month.

Five emails in total, unsigned and from a strange email address. All professing love and written in haiku.

It was creepy.

She knew the other women who had shared her ticket had similar problems regarding the media—it was an extra reason she was grateful they had decided to stick together, and even more reason that they were all anxious to finally be moving into their new apartments that week.

The frigid January wind seemed to find every possible opening in her coat as she exited the children's clothing store in the strip mall. One of the female customers had whispered to her companion while they both darted looks in Meena's direction. Her lack of privacy had been worsened by the posters with their picture on them that had been posted around town at all the lottery tickets sale locations the previous summer. Thankfully they had started disappearing from windows before Christmas, so she wasn't getting recognized as often. These ladies must have *really* good memories.

She thought, not for the first time, that what she really wanted was to go back on the cruise ship and the balmy Caribbean weather they had enjoyed a few weeks ago. Maybe it would have been more practical to upgrade her car first and take the cruise second, but they had all needed to get away. No one there had known who she or her shelter sisters were, and the only attention she received from guys was because they liked the way she looked, not the size of her wallet. Sadly, she couldn't be sure that was the case with any of the men who hit on her in Crystal Creek, Kansas.

She didn't need to buy Deven new clothes desperately enough to deal with pointing and whispers today. Maybe Dierdre had the right idea with shopping online. They were moving tomorrow to their new building and new clothes would just be more to pack, anyway. Right? So much for taking a couple of hours away to run errands and unwind.

Getting into her beat-up, but still functional car—she would look at upgrading when she knew how much their building renovations was going to eat up from her winnings and they were sure there weren't going to be any major surprises from the tax man—Meena headed to the U-Haul office to pick up more boxes, and then back home to finish preparing for the move. Might as well get it out of the way.

She wrinkled her nose as she walked down the musty hallway, but smiled when Andrea opened her door. Until she spoke.

"Apparently there's a new commercial starring *us* that just came out. Dierdre saw it earlier today. Do you have more boxes you need brought up?"

"This is all I bought this time—nearly done. I picked up a few extra in case anyone else needs some." She shifted the boxes to get a better grip. "I guess the new commercial explains why I was recognized at the kid's store. I've always loved people who point and stare, it makes me feel so special."

Andrea smiled, knowing exactly how annoying it was. "Could be they just don't see an Indian beauty often enough here in the land of the whites."

Meena just chuckled. "Do you guys need any boxes?"

"One more should do me. Sheila could probably use a couple too." Andrea adjusted the vibrant cloth she had used to tie back her tight black curls so they wouldn't get coated with dirt in the packing. A smudge of dust ran across her rich brown skin. "I just heard from the cleaning crew—our apartments are ready. They're finishing up your new office and we'll be good to go. They'll be here by eleven tomorrow to clean out the ones here once our stuff is out."

"Okay, so I was just thinking that being recognized everywhere is a major pain, but seriously, being able to hire someone else to do that deep cleaning is a nice perk."

"You're telling me." Andrea took the three boxes Meena had peeled away from the rest. "Let me know if you need more help with the last of your things."

A man walked past them, eying them both with the strange distrust that several of their neighbors had shown since they won the American Lotto.

"Will do. I'm seriously ready to get out of here." Meena hoisted up the stack of boxes again and headed down three more doors to her apartment.

"Oh, good. I just used the last one. Deven's still sleeping." Bennett had her blond curls pulled back in a ponytail that made her look more like eighteen than twenty-four and wore an older gray tee that read "If You Believe In Telekinesis Please Raise My Hand."

"I guess playing the packing game before I left wore him out," Meena said.

"Andrea said we could bring him over later if we need to. Also, did you get Dierdre's text? She's hosting dinner tonight." They had taken turns making dinner the past few days so everyone could pack, and so they had an excuse to get together to talk logistics and get construction updates on their new building.

"Bless her."

"What do you want done with your meditation corner?" Bennett pointed to the praying hands, lotus blossoms, and small statue of Krishna that Meena sat in front of to meditate every morning and night—one of the Indian traditions she had taken with her when her parents disowned her.

"I'll pack them in the morning after meditation. I saved a smaller box under my pillow for that."

"Ah, I wondered why you were hoarding that."

The two of them couldn't look any different—Bennett was compact and curvy with shoulder-length blond curls, peaches and cream skin, and green eyes. Meena was tall and thin with almost no curves—well, a few more since having Deven—and the dark hair, eyes and complexion of her Indian ancestors. They even had different belief systems, but they couldn't be closer if they were sisters by blood.

"Andrea said we're starring in a new lotto commercial, which explains the renewed pointing and staring I experienced today." Meena opened an upper cupboard and packed the end of their food, except for some breakfast bars for the next morning.

"Face it, you're gorgeous and you stand out. People would point and stare anyway."

An alarm went off on Bennett's phone. "School's out soon. My turn to pick up the girls. Be back. Think of me as you dig through the summer clothes closet next."

"Right." Somehow their off-season items always managed to get mixed together, which wasn't a major problem when they lived in the same apartment, but they would be getting their own the next day, so sorting was a must. Of course, since they would be next door to each other, it wouldn't exactly be difficult to return items if they were packed in the wrong box.

"Mommy, I'm hungry." Deven called from their shared room. She smiled as she realized she wouldn't have to share a bed or even a bedroom with her son anymore after that night. Luxury.

Okay, maybe being a millionaire wasn't so bad.

# Three

MOVING DAY. IT WOULDN'T be the final move into their newly renovated apartments on the top floors since there would be months more before those were ready, but at least they would be getting out of the dump where the six of them had been living for the past two to three years and into the only slightly less dumpy, but much more secure building that they now owned. Renovations on the building had progressed enough that the second-floor apartments they would be temporarily moving into had been repainted and the windows were replaced—that would do until the fall when they should be moving upstairs.

The first of the building's two new elevators had been installed, leading from the new side entrance to the second and third floor which would someday be condos.

Meena had finished packing her meditation

corner when Deven ran into the room carrying the photo album Chris had made for their unborn child shortly before he died in combat in Afghanistan three years earlier. "Pictures!" he exclaimed, holding it out to her.

She knew what that meant. She glanced at the clock, and decided she could spare a few minutes to review the pictures for the hundredth time that month—it was ragged and about to fall apart. She would have to get a new mini album to put the photos in soon.

They opened the book and looked through the photos. Grandma and Grandpa Bertrand. Auntie Casey. Daddy. Mommy. Daddy and Kaleb. Mommy and Daddy. Auntie Emry and Uncle Jake.

Meena kept turning the pages, pointing out faces while Deven called out the names he had memorized long ago. She flipped past the image of her own parents without letting Deven see it and then paused for Deven to identify the people in the next shot.

"Mommy, Daddy, Kabe," he lisped.

"Right. Mommy, Daddy, Kaleb."

He helped her flip the page, but that was the last picture, so he closed the book.

Meena pressed a kiss to his cheek. "Can you put the pictures in the box over there?" She pointed to the one she had been packing.

Deven ran over and put the book inside.

Now all she had to do was fold up the sheets from the bed she and Deven had slept in, get ready for the day, and throw the final items in the very last box before the movers arrived. She could hardly wait.

There was a knock at her door as she let Deven "help" her seal the box with the vibrant red packing tape that designated her things. Bennett had already left to take the four elementary school aged girls to class for the day. Meena checked the peephole in the door and saw Andrea on the other side. She opened it with a wiggle of excitement. "Hey, you ready for this?"

"So ready I can taste it, sister. Bennett said you were good to go."

"I just have to switch the fridge stuff into a box before we lock up for the last time. Is Comfrey still willing to watch our three little monsters for a few hours?"

"Yes, I'll take the boys over in twenty minutes." Andrea let out a sigh of happiness.

This was really happening. Meena could hardly believe it, even after the months of preparation and planning, it had somehow not seemed real.

The movers arrived at nine on the dot and started emptying Sheila and Andrea's apartment first. Each box, bag, or piece of furniture was tagged with a color for the corresponding person so the movers could drop the items in the correct apartments when they got to the new building. Meena hoped the system would work. Having all six of them use the same moving vans was more cost effective, and meant they would all get to move at the same time.

Three and a half hours later as the movers brought the last few boxes down the hall to Andrea's new apartment, Meena took a moment to walk through her new place. Her *own* apartment. Bennett lived through the thin walls in the next apartment, but this space was all hers, along with the empty one across the hall where she would set up her jewelry-making equipment. From the time she had entered the hospital with preeclampsia nearly three years earlier, she hadn't had space that was solely hers. First there was the roommate at the hospital and frequent interruptions by staff, then the women's shelter, and then she and Bennett had moved in together to share the child-rearing and expense responsibilities. Now she had this apartment *and* the one across the hall for business. Even if they weren't large or in any way fancy, she didn't mind. They were hers!

The sound of hammering came up through the floor from the construction crews working on the first floor which would soon become a retail store, office space, a pool, parking garage, and Sheila's welding studio.

Deirdre followed the movers back downstairs to lock up and Sheila called the rest of the women to meet in the halls.

"This place is a dump." Vanna, the sixth and final woman in their group, brushed the back of her wrist over her sweaty forehead, nudging her blond hair out of the way. She was usually so polished and professional looking, it was kind of funny seeing her in sweats and a t-shirt.

"Yes, but it's *our* dump," Bennett said. "And give it a year or two—no one will be calling it a dump anymore. We just have to survive construction for that long."

"Bad news," Deirdre said as she stepped off the elevator. "I got a call from the window guys, there was an incident at their current project and they aren't going to be able to finish the upper floors for a couple more *weeks.*"

"Heating that space with the old windows is going to cost a mint." Andrea shot her a frown, as if Deirdre was responsible for the holdup.

"It can't be helped. At least we have a solid roof over our heads and the bottom floors have new windows." Bennett shoved her hands in her pockets. "Hopefully the windows will arrive before the framers move up there."

"We can always dream."

"All right, enough with the news. Anyone else starving? DeQuan's is now only a three-minute walk away," Sheila reminded them. "We have another hour of babysitting and two before the girls get out of school. I say we celebrate."

Everyone agreed and they headed for the stairs.

"I wonder if we could convince them to deliver sometimes." Bennett was slightly addicted to the Chinese restaurant. "I know they don't normally, but we're so *close* now."

"We just need to convince them to hire someone to do deliveries." Vanna pulled her honey blond hair from the elastic it had been falling out of and scooped it all back into a fresh ponytail. Despite the casual, no-mirror effort, it looked great because Vanna seemed incapable of anything less.

Meena pushed her hair envy back down and was glad she had checked her own ponytail in the mirror a few minutes ago.

"DeQuan's has been upping their game with the new paint job. If enough people ask for it, maybe they'll break down and do it," Andrea said hopefully.

"If they started delivering, I'd be getting fat." Dierdre was the first to the bottom of the stairs and came to stop by the outside door.

"Whatever. You could use a little more meat on your bones." Andrea pinched Dierdre's pale, skinny arms.

"Hey, hands off the goods. All right, time to go over the security system—then we can grab lunch." Dierdre had a way with electronics and had set up each of their apartments with a buzzer from the street so they would know if someone was at the door for them. There was a high-tech security system for all of the entrances on the main floor, including video surveillance they could all access, and she had added alarms to all the windows on their floor as well to make sure people didn't try to break in. It gave Meena a sense of peace considering some of the weirdness that had gone on in the old place.

The buzzer pad outside didn't have their names, only numbers one through six on them. Dierdre had covered all kinds of contingencies, leaving Meena wondering where she had learned some of this stuff. They had covered the computer end of things already, but now Dierdre showed them how to use the keypad outside and passed out their badges.

Meena slipped the card into her back pocket for now, glad it was a key card-plus-pin setup in case someone had their card stolen. All set, they continued walking to the restaurant, which was only a few hundred feet away.

They hardly ever got to eat a meal with just the six women—they almost always had the boys with them since they were still toddlers. Not that Meena didn't love all seven kids—every one of whom she had taken turns watching numerous times—but sometimes you just needed girl time. Being the only ones in their apartment building would hopefully lead to a lot more girl time after the kids were in bed.

"I think that was the easiest move, ever," Andrea said as they were walking past the community garden that separated them from the Chinese restaurant.

"Ha, ha. We still have to unpack our things," Sheila reminded her.

"It's not like any of us have all that much to unpack," Dierdre said. "I can't wait to get my new equipment set up and start making soap again. I had a custom order come through a few days ago and you know how long it takes to cure."

"And I have some scarf designs screaming to be released." Bennett made the most beautiful hand-felted scarves as well as insanely soft hand-dyed wool yarn.

"I've been working on a design for the new stair rail. If I find my notebook, I'll show you all tonight. It's going to be beautiful." Sheila had been designing wrought iron decorations for about a year and had been chomping at the bit to replace the railing in what would become their private stairwell once they moved to the upper floors. "My ventilation system should be here in a couple of days and my other tools are arriving tomorrow. I can hardly wait." She had been slowing collecting equipment over the past year, but still borrowed several items from another metal artist in nearby Leavenworth.

They ordered their food and crammed into a corner booth. "So, the blond mover was cute. Anyone interested?" Vanna asked.

"Are you asking because you want to hook one of us up, or because you want to know if the way is clear for yourself?" Bennett asked.

"Oh, you guys, all the way. I was thinking Meena, actually. He watched you every time you were nearby. Definite interest." Vanna wiggled her brows—a matchmaker by trade, she was always trying to hook someone up.

"No thanks, I have enough on my plate without bringing a guy into the mix." Besides, knowing he was watching her gave her the creeps—he could even be the guy sending her emails. No thanks.

"Anyone else? Come on, my clientele is growing way too slow. You're all eligible ladies. Tell me you want me to hook you up—Andrea, I met a really nice guy for you. He's not exactly Mr. Right, but you could stand to get out and have a little fun."

"You'll have to keep your matchmaking business to clients only," Andrea said.

"All in favor say Aye," Bennett said.

A chorus of ayes went up.

"Fine. But honestly, love with the right guy is worth everything. You just have to find Mr. Right. I'll focus on my clients instead. For now." Vanna pulled a face at them.

Meena believed her, but everything she needed friendship-wise was around this table.

# Four

THE ROCK AND GEM SHOP in Leavenworth was one of Meena's favorite places to visit. Now that she had money to buy nicer specimens for her jewelry projects, she made a point of going in whenever she could. It smelled like dust, lavender, and possibilities.

"Hi, George, how are things going today?" she asked the proprietor, who had to be at least eighty years old.

"Fit as a fiddle. What can I do for you today, darling?" He had one of those grandfatherly faces and demeanors that made everyone feel at home.

"I have a client who wants some earrings with pink stones or crystals dangling off the bottom. Do you have anything small enough to work?"

"I think I do. Over there where Charlie's working right now." He gestured to his grandson, a dark-haired man in his mid-twenties.

"I can help you out if you know what you need now. Pink is popular." Charlie spoke hesitantly as usual, a remnant, she supposed, of the accident George had said Charlie had been in over the summer. Charlie opened the door on his side of the display and pulled out a tray of pink stones from quartz to rhodonite to red agate.

"These are nice." She fingered some round beads in rose quartz that would be far too big for the earrings unless the woman liked having her ears scream in agony. "I'll take seven for a bracelet. Also," her finger shifted to the red agate, which were darker, but a smaller circumference. "These four little ones will be perfect for the earrings." They had good color and no imperfections as she rolled them on the velvet-lined tray.

"Is that all you need? We have many other stones. You might like a few."

"Maybe I will look for a few other things." She poked around the store for twenty minutes, picking out items here or there and finally grabbing a stack of magnetic stones to use to hang her designs in her new studio.

She left the store with a wave goodbye and headed back to her car, which she had parked around the corner on Cherokee Street.

She heard footsteps approaching behind her and

male voices talking. "So I told Kirby to forget it; I'd just grab it myself."

"He should know better by now than to try to pin you down," another man said. His voice was smooth, slightly Texan, and very familiar.

Wanting to get a look at the speaker without looking like a gawker, Meena glanced back as she turned at the corner and nearly dropped her jaw in shock when she realized her ears hadn't deceived her. "Kaleb?"

His head swiveled to look in her direction and he stopped before he could take another step. He looked exactly like the last time she had seen him in his desert camo fatigues, close-cropped blond hair that liked to curl when it grew even a little, and impossibly blue eyes that had always seemed to see right through her. "Meena?"

A moment later she was crushed in his arms. "What are you doing here?" he asked. "I tried to find you on Facebook but you haven't been there or your other social media pages in ages and I had no idea where you ended up. I even looked for you at your old apartment a few days ago when I had a day off. I was about to call in the cavalry to see if we could track you down. How's the baby?"

Meena laughed, hugging him back and appreciating the pine scent of his cologne. He had been her husband's best friend, sticking together from freshman year in college, into the Army and paratrooper training. Where Chris was, Kaleb was at his side. She had missed him so much. "He's not exactly a baby anymore, and he's doing great. You wouldn't believe how big Deven is."

Kaleb had always been an enormous man, wide shouldered and a good eight inches taller than she was—and with muscles popping out all over. Chris, on the other hand, had been well muscled, but leaner and a few inches shorter. She reveled in the hug—his had always been superior, making her feel totally accepted. Considering how he had distanced himself from her a few months before he and Chris had deployed, though, she hadn't expected such a warm reception if she ever saw him again.

"Deven, I remember that was on your short list of names. I want to see him." He pulled back and looked at her. "I've wondered how you were every day. Your phone was disconnected when I tried it, and you just seemed to drop off the face of the planet. You look amazing as always."

"You look great, too. I went through a rough patch after Chris died, but I'm doing really good now."

He picked up her free hand and regret slid onto his face. "I'm so *sorry* I wasn't here for you. I always wondered what happened to you. We have to catch up."

A throat cleared behind him.

"Oh, right." He released her and shifted back to gesture to the man behind him. "This is Nash, aka Sgt. Peters. Nash, this is Meena."

"Nice to meet you, ma'am." Nash reminded his friend, "Remember I have to be back at my duty station in fifteen minutes."

"Crap. Of all the days. Give me a minute." He didn't take his eyes from Meena as he answered his friend, then shifted his conversation back to her. "Please tell me you live locally and aren't just visiting or something."

"I live in Crystal Creek, which is less than ten miles away. I come here sometimes to pick up supplies."

"Can I get your number? I want to see that godson of mine and catch up."

She took the phone out of his hands and flipped to the directory app. "Godson? Where did you get that idea?"

"Chris and I decided that when he first heard you were pregnant. Sorry, you have no choice." He said it good-naturedly enough, showing a hint of the smile that had always warmed her.

"I guess not." Meena chuckled as she entered her

phone number. Seeing Kaleb brought equal parts pleasure and pain, but it had been so long since she had been able to talk to him. It hadn't occurred to her that he would still be wondering about her—he had given up trying to contact her soon enough after Chris died, while she had been out of contact. "Are you stationed here?" She sent herself a quick text message so she would have his number.

"Yes, and that's a long story for another day." He took his phone back. "I'll text you and we'll see what works for our schedules." He glanced at his watch. "I really do have to get going."

They stared at each other for several seconds before he spoke again. "Seriously, I'm so glad we ran into each other. I'll talk to you soon."

"Good." She was glad, but also really confused, and then there were the final memories of him and Chris before they shipped out—memories which hadn't been sweet, though apparently he didn't remember it the same way.

He gave her a little wave and then hurried off with his friend.

Meena, wishing she had somewhere to sit down, crossed to her car and sat inside it for a long moment while she got her emotions under control. Seeing Kaleb was surreal—both painful and energizing at the same time.

Knowing she didn't have time to wallow there in the cold, she started the engine—she needed to get home to watch the little boys while some of the others walked across the street to pick up the older kids from school or spent time setting up their work spaces.

As she walked up the stairs at home a while later, her phone beeped. She pulled it out of her pocket as Bennett approached. Today's shirt read "That's Too Much Bacon—Said No One Ever."

Kaleb: **Dinner tomorrow night? Six? Bring Deven and we'll go somewhere kid friendly.**

Meena: **I have just the place in mind.**

"Who's that?" Bennett asked.

"Chris' friend Kaleb."

"Who? Oh, wait—Kaleb, the one from Deven's photo album?"

"That's the one. I ran into him in Leavenworth today. I guess he's stationed there now."

"Well, well. And he's already texting you?"

"We're going to dinner tomorrow, so he can get to know Deven."

"Right... It's for Deven. I get it." She zipped up her coat. "I'm on pickup duty. You should check in on your squirt; he's been asking about you."

"Thanks, you're the best." Meena went to the common room where everyone could gather when they wanted to be social, or to watch several kids at the same time without having all of the chaos in their personal apartments, and Deven ran into her arms—the perfect combination of her Indian coloring and his father's European ancestry.

"Mommy, Mommy. I missed you!" he said with the slight lisp so common in toddlers.

"Hey there, baby. How are you?" She listened as he babbled about playing with Parker and Bobby, nodding and making appropriate expressions of amazement in the correct places.

Still, she couldn't entirely block out thoughts about Kaleb. She hadn't even thought of him in months, maybe over a year, but despite the way things had ended last time, she was looking forward to getting to know him again.

As Deven's godfather, of course.

Within thirty minutes all of the moms had picked up their kids for homework or quiet time before dinner. Meena followed suit, keeping her apartment door closed until after dinner, needing some quiet time to get some business paperwork done as well as pick apart Kaleb's every word and action that afternoon. No question that he was happy to see her and didn't seem to feel the awkwardness of their past, but that might come back when they sat down to eat together. Had she been too hasty in accepting his invitation? It wasn't like he'd been someone she could count on. Once she had thought that he was, but it turned out that he was only there for Chris.

By the time she got Deven into bed, she was ready to talk to some adults and get out of her own head for a while.

"Hey, you've been all tucked into your shell tonight," Andrea said when Meena came into the common apartment. She was the last one there— apparently everyone else had the same idea as she did.

"Sorry, end-of-year taxes to file, two new items to load to Etsy and an inventory order to put through. I also added some items to our shopping app. How about all of you?" She was good at brooding while still being efficient.

"Homework, dinner, fighting over the evening shower and finally bedtime. Come join us," Dierdre said. "I'll do the shopping run tomorrow if anyone else wants to add things to the app."

"Have you told them yet, about the hottie?" Bennett asked Meena as she joined them in the room.

"What hottie?" Andrea demanded. "There's a hottie? Why haven't you told us yet?"

Meena shot Bennett a dirty look. "I haven't had a chance to tell them about Kaleb." She looked back to Andrea, and all of the other curious faces. "I was shopping in Leavenworth earlier, picking up stones for some projects."

"Of course," Andrea said.

"Is he an Army hottie? I know you go for that type," Vanna referenced Chris.

"Yes. But he's actually Chris' best friend, so technically I didn't just *meet* him. I've known him for a long time."

"He just *happens* to be posted here, and you just *happened* to run into him when you were in town, which you hardly ever are? Doesn't it sound a little too coincidental?" Dierdre had always been the most paranoid of the group.

"Well, maybe when you put it like that, but it seemed totally innocent and reasonable. It's not like I was in some random non-Army town when I ran into him. Chris always said the Army isn't as big as people think it is. He sometimes ran into people he knew from boot camp or from his hometown when he was deployed." Was she trying to convince herself? They would see through that in a heartbeat.

"They have a date tomorrow night." Bennett was all about sharing today. Apparently.

"Seriously? How well did you know him?" Dierdre's eyes narrowed.

"Yeah, don't jump into anything," Sheila advised.

"Well enough." And not as well as she had once

thought. "Look, can we table this? I'm not sure it's really a date. I mean, he's Deven's godfather and wants to see him, ergo, dinner because I'm not ready to bring him back here to meet all of you."

"Godfather? But you're Hindu," Dierdre said.

"Yes, but Chris and Kaleb were...are...whatever, both Catholic, so...godfather. Besides, it's a beautiful tradition, having a friend who's there to help you raise your child to be an upright human being. I mean, I have all of you, but that doesn't mean that it won't be good for Deven to have a male role model. Besides, when Kaleb gets his next assignment, he could be off to a different corner of the world, so it's not like he's always going to be around, and Deven deserves to have a man who cares about him. At least for a while. And he's a good man." She had missed him when he started pulling away, coming around less in the months before he and Chris had been deployed on that fatal assignment. He had still hung out with her husband, just not much when she was in the vicinity.

"What are you going to wear?" Vanna asked, passing over a Diet Coke.

"Are you going to even be able to find your clothes in all those boxes?" Bennett added. "Why haven't you unpacked all of your clothes, anyway?"

"There aren't that many boxes left to go, and my clothes will be fine. I'll find something." She popped open the soda can and took a drink so she wouldn't have to talk anymore. Honestly, she was nervous about seeing Kaleb again and talking to him. Worried about how he would respond when he found out about everything that had happened since he saw her last. Would he blame her for the homelessness that had brought her to these women after Chris had died? Would he think less of her because of the struggles she had gone through?

"So, spill, tell us everything about him," Andrea prompted.

Meena shrugged off her discomfort and filled in a few sketchy details. She could always add more later if it was warranted. After this one night, he may decide he *still* didn't want anything to do with her.

These women were her best friends, sisters even, but that didn't mean she couldn't have any secrets.

# Five

KALEB FELT LIKE A SIXTEEN-year-old going on a first date, which was ridiculous. It wasn't even a date. Not really. After all, Deven would be there—that was his name, right? Chris died before his son was born—Meena had only just found out that it was a boy when Chris died. Then a couple of weeks after the funeral, she seemed to just drop off the face of the earth. He'd been stuck in Afghanistan, so he hadn't been able to track her down in person.

Deven would be there tonight, he repeated to himself, so that made it an outing, not a date.

Not that he would be opposed to a date. Except it was Chris' *wife*. Widow.

He shook his head as he approached the six-story apartment building displaying the address she had given him. He parked on the road and then headed around the west side of the building to the side door and pushed the call button simply labeled "1".

Her voice came through the speaker. "Hi, Kaleb. Just a sec, we'll be right down."

He was surprised she had been so sure it would be him. Was it that unusual for her to get visitors? How many people lived here? Based on the enormous dumpster set in the parking lot behind the building, he had to guess that the building was getting a face lift. How many people could possibly be living here if there were no cars parked out back, or in front? Where did she park her car?

The door opened and Meena peeked out, her dark almond eyes crinkled at the edges as she smiled at him. "Don't you look handsome in your civvies?" She adjusted her large purse over her shoulder and tugged the hand of her three-year-old son who was trying to run away. Deven had her eyes and coloring, and Chris' mouth and nose. It should have been an odd combination, but it wasn't.

"I admit, it's nice to be able to dress in normal clothes now that I'm back in the US. I've spent too many years in Afghanistan and living in camo. Did you just guess that it was me on the intercom?"

"Oh, no." She pointed at a well-concealed camera off to the side of the entrance. "I checked the camera feed when you rang the bell."

"Fancy." He hunched down to talk to the kid. "You must be Deven. Hey, buddy."

Deven grinned. "Kabe!"

"Kaleb, good job. You know my name." He shot Meena a questioning look.

"Almost every day we go through the little book of pictures that Chris put together for me. There are a few of you in it. Apparently, Chris wanted his baby to know his godfather as well as himself."

"I had totally forgotten about that. You ready?"

"Yeah."

He wanted to take her hand, but decided that was way too forward, so he slid his hands in his coat pockets instead. "You said you know a good place for dinner?"

"Yeah, it's casual enough to bring a kid, has great dishes for the meat eaters, and some nice vegetarian options. We should take my car—he needs a car seat."

"Sounds good."

"What are you doing at Fort Leavenworth—have you shifted to military police duty?" She led the way around the building to a back door and pulled a key card from her pocket, lifting it to the scanner and adding a numeric code. His brows lifted in surprise at the security precautions.

"No, actually. I'm here working in Foreign Military Studies, which is basically putting together reports and brochures that go out to the troops." He was surprised to see only six cars parked in the garage—

none of them particularly fancy. There was another door to the inside beyond the cars with a similar key reader and touchpad.

"That sounds, um, interesting."

He chuckled as she stopped at a worn-out tan sedan, unlocking the door manually with a key. "Sometimes, but mostly it's just nice having regular hours in a normal nine-to-five job. How many people live in this apartment building?"

"Just the six families for now. After renovations are all complete, there will be a bunch more moving in. It's been empty for a while."

"Are you staying in a renovated area?"

"No, we're all on the second floor for now. The renovations are on the first, fourth, fifth and sixth. They'll get around to the second and third later. How long are you staying in the area?"

"Two years."

Meena looked up from where she was buckling Deven into his seat. "Really? That's great. You said you hadn't been here very long, right?"

"About three weeks, so most of my time is ahead of me. I was really hoping I'd be able to find you when I was offered this assignment. After you weren't active on Facebook or Instagram anymore I worried that something had happened to you."

"Well, I'm not going anywhere now."

He wanted to press for more details, but she was moving around to the driver's door and he hurried to open it for her.

Once they were both seated, Meena pushed the garage door button and backed into the empty slot across from her and then pulled into the outdoor parking lot.

"It seems like an awfully large building for such a small lot."

"Yeah, it was slummy housing before and a lot of the tenants couldn't afford a car. We...the garage just got added this fall. Everything is going to become condo housing—larger ones for families instead of tiny cracker boxes, and the plan is to add some covered parking spaces in the outside lot. There's a lot of growth in Crystal Creek right now."

"In the meantime, you get to enjoy the dubious perks of living with construction?"

"Yeah. At least it's private on our floor." She focused on the road, heading north.

She asked him several questions about his family and his quarters on base. Every time he tried to ask her questions, she demurred and turned it back on him until they were seated in the locally-owned family restaurant and had ordered their food.

"Okay, now that you've found out everything about me," Chris said, "What happened to you? I haven't heard anything or been able to find out where you were since Chris' funeral. I wondered if you'd moved home or something."

She smiled, though it looked more rueful than happy. "Now there's a story."

The waitress stopped by with rolls and butter and Meena took her own sweet time buttering part of one for Deven and the rest for herself before continuing. "Are you sure you want the whole messy disaster right now?"

"Two or three messy disasters if you have them."

She seemed to think for a moment. "There were several, but I'll focus on the main one for now."

There were several disasters? She seemed to be doing fine now, for what it was worth, even if she was living in a dump. A dump with lots of security which was intriguing. He hated the idea of her dealing with Chris' death all by herself, yet he knew her family hadn't been at all happy about the marriage. Though he felt the compulsion to rub his fingers over hers, he reined it in. Instead he busied his hands with his roll.

Taking a deep breath, she started. "A few weeks after the funeral, I started to have some problems with the pregnancy. The doctors said it was stress, probably because of Chris' death, but that was only one of the *many* crazy things happening in my life right then. My employer and I came to an impasse and I stopped working there, there were some issues with the funeral home, my friend that I moved out here to be near decided she couldn't handle my drama after all, and Chris' family pulled back after his death, despite knowing about Deven."

"You're kidding me." He had known Chris' family for years and didn't understand why they wouldn't want regular contact with his child.

"Nope. Not that they have cut us off completely—for the most part they've been happy to get pictures of their *little brown dumpling*, as his mom calls Deven, but they're not interested in actually seeing us."

Brown dumpling? What had Chris' mom been thinking? "I had no idea things had gotten so bad, especially with Chris' family. When I asked them about you, they just said they hadn't heard from you for a while and didn't know where you were now. I'm just blown away that they did that."

"Oh, come on, they weren't at *all* happy that I married their darling Chris to begin with. I think they weren't sure what to do about the fact that I would be raising my son alone, Hindu. That I believe in sharing his father's culture with him as well would never have occurred to them."

He felt terrible that she had gone through all of that and he hadn't known about it. "So, you were having issues with the pregnancy and then what happened?"

Meena took a moment to pick up the crayons that Deven had pushed onto the seat beside them. She gave him another piece of roll and the crayon before turning back to Kaleb. "I ended up in the ER and the doctor prescribed total bed rest. That went on for a couple of months with my landlord pounding on the door for rent, which I didn't have. Then I was in the hospital for a couple of weeks. While I was recovering from the birth, and visiting Deven who was in the NICU for nearly three weeks, I got kicked out of my apartment for non-payment, and the hospital bills kept climbing."

"But you have insurance through the Army and benefits..."

"Yeah, well, there were some problems with those because Chris wasn't so good with paperwork. I had started to get bills back on the prenatal visits, and he swore he'd get it fixed, but he never got around to it. Oh, and did I mention that not having money meant my phone and internet got turned off—thus why you couldn't reach me. It took months to straighten out everything."

This got worse at every turn. "What did you do?"

"Someone I met at the hospital was from Crystal Creek and knew the director of the women's shelter here in town. I knew I wouldn't have to stay for too long—I just needed to get things cleared up with Chris' benefits and then I could get out on my own again. So that's what I did."

The waitress came, interrupting the conversation long enough to set down the plates and ask if they needed anything more.

Kaleb was grateful for the break, horrified to know everything Meena had gone through—the guilt of Chris' death had been bad enough before, but now, knowing how badly things had gone for her... He could hardly look her in the eye. He wasn't a weakling, though, so he lifted his gaze to meet hers. "I am so sorry all of that happened to you. That I couldn't be here for you. Why didn't you reach out to me when all of this was going on?"

Meena cleared away the crayons and cut up Deven's chicken and vegetables into bite-sized pieces talking to him and answering questions so long that Kaleb thought he would have to ask her again.

Apparently, she remembered where they had left off because she continued on as if there had been no interruption. "You were in Afghanistan, what could you have done? Besides, I knew you had to be at least as devastated by Chris' death as I was, and you had distanced yourself, so I didn't feel like I could rely on you."

He wondered for a moment if she was aware of the guilt he felt, of his part in Chris' death, but her gaze held no censure. If he told her everything, how quickly would her feelings change to something far less accepting? He pushed that thought back and tried to focus on the rest of her story. He had to have it all. "How long were you in the women's shelter? Was it awful?"

"It wasn't awful. I mean, it was a shelter, so it wasn't cushy, but it was a nice place, and the director was very helpful in hooking me up with the right people to push through the paperwork for Chris' benefits. She found me an advocate who helped get most of the remaining medical bills forgiven after the insurance took their part. The portion that was left was cut up into manageable bites. And I met Bennett there, which made everything a hundred times more doable."

"Bennett?" Oh no, there was another guy in her life. He should have been happy that she had found someone else so fast, but couldn't quite manage it. Not yet. He hoped his face didn't show his reaction.

"We moved in together, to help each other with childcare and bills. She had been at the shelter for a couple of months before I got there."

*She.* Bennett was a she. Right, Meena had said that it was a women's shelter. He had forgotten that for a moment. Crisis averted. And why was it a crisis?

He and Meena were only friends, after all. "I'm glad you found someone to help you."

She played with her dinner and smiled. "I found five people to help me, support me, and generally just get through everything. They and their kids became my family."

Something niggled in his head. "Wait, five? As in the other five families who live in your building?"

"Yes."

"How did that happen?"

"That's a whole other story, not full of terrible issues." She smiled a little as she forked up some stir-fried peppers.

Fair enough—he hadn't earned her trust again yet. He would fix that soon enough. He definitely wanted to know more about the women's shelter. "And you're happy? You look happy."

"I'm very happy. I have my own place now, my shelter sisters are close, and I'm back to making and selling jewelry—without my annoying boss looking over my shoulder and getting huffy when my designs sold at his store."

"Really? I'd love to see some of your pieces."

She held out her hands and pointed to three of the four rings she wore, describing the stones and when she had made them.

"I bow down to your expertise. It's beautiful

49

work." He had seen a couple of photos of her work that she had sent to Chris before, but they hadn't done her pieces justice.

"Thank you. I've been so happy since I've been able to quit my old job and focus on making jewelry full time." Meena used a paper napkin to wipe the sauce from Deven's face and handed him the fork again, since he had released it in favor of eating with his hands. "Use your fork, sweetie."

Kaleb picked up a thick steak-cut fry and dipped it in barbecue sauce he'd poured on the edge of his plate. "Where do you sell it? Making it full time is incredible. You've come a long way from living at the shelter."

"Yes I have. I have an Etsy shop, and some of us are creating a joint store to sell the various things we make. It's going to be great. Tell me about the last place you were stationed. Your tour in Afghanistan should have ended a long time ago."

"Oh, that first one did, but then they sent me right back out there—just to a different area." He filled in some sketchy details over dinner, picking out a couple of stories to share that he thought would make her laugh, even though they weren't exactly representative of his time there.

Between taking care of Deven and bites of food, Meena laughed in all the right places and Kaleb admired the way her eyes lit up when she was genuinely laughing. He could get used to this. He felt a resurgence of the attraction that had drawn him to her the night that they had very first met—but then Chris did everything in his power to weave Meena under his spell. He had succeeded, too, much to Kaleb's disappointment.

"Where did you go just now?" Meena asked when they had both been silent for a long moment.

"Sorry, I was just thinking about the night we first met. Chris was his usual, charming self."

Her smile weakened. "If you don't mind, could we put off that particular trip down memory lane for another night?"

"Of course." Maybe he had worn out his welcome. She didn't seem in a hurry to end the meal, but he could be wrong.

Deven, on the other hand, was ready to get out of his seat. Kaleb signaled to the waitress, who quickly brought the check. "Do you want to go somewhere else to let him run around for a bit, or do you need to get him home to bed?"

Meena checked the time on her phone. "It's nearly his bedtime, and it's too cold to run around after dark."

"Right, of course." He felt like an idiot. Maybe she really was trying to get rid of him.

"Oh, but we need to get together again soon. The weather's going to be bad for a while, but maybe next week?"

Relief poured through him. "Yes, definitely. I'll check back with you after these storms have passed through." He had never lived in Kansas or Missouri in the winter, but one of the guys at the base had mentioned that winter storms like the series predicted for the next four days often left the roads impassable from ice even when they dumped little or no snow.

When they exited the car in her garage, she headed for the outside door instead of the door that led into the building. "Why don't you go in the other way?"

"There's no connection to my floor through the garage right now. Renovations. The only way up to the second floor is the side door."

"Oh, all right then."

He was curious about her apartment—could she really be doing well enough with her Etsy store to stay in such a secure building? Was it as safe as it looked?

They stopped at the side entrance and stood in the porch light for a moment. He held a very tired Deven in his arms. Meena reached for him. Kaleb wanted to offer to take Deven to her apartment, but her body language said that wouldn't be happening so he compromised. "At least get the door open before you take him. Looks like you might need an extra hand for that."

"Oh, yeah. Thanks." She used the key card and code to get the door open and nudged it with her foot, so it wouldn't close on her before turning back to take Deven. "It was really great seeing you again."

"It really was. I'll call or text." The little boy seemed way too big for her tiny frame to carry, but as Kaleb stepped back, he realized she had been carrying her boy for a long time, pretty much on her own. He hoped he could ease that burden a little. That was the least he could do.

"Good night."

She echoed the phrase back and moved away. The door came to a firm close behind her. Wanting to be sure, he gave it an extra tug, then nodded before heading to his car.

MEENA HEADED FOR the elevator, glad she didn't have to lug more than thirty pounds of little boy up the flight of stairs. It was so good to see Kaleb again. After he had distanced himself from her three years ago, she had started to wonder if the genuinely nice guy, the rolling laugh, and insightful way he had always seemed to know what to say to her, had been her imagination. The only thing missing this time around was the laughing eyes that had defined him before. Of course, she'd expected serving in the Middle East to change him. He'd been in a battle zone for more than three years—how could she expect him to be exactly the same? But how could she not mourn the loss of his bright happiness?

When the elevator doors opened on the second floor, Dierdre was waiting for her.

"What a hunk. You didn't mention he was that good looking."

Meena shot her a look of exasperation. "What, did you have the monitor sitting in front of you, waiting for me to come home?"

"Not exactly, but the feed was in my line of sight. I wondered if he would try out some moves on you."

"It's Kaleb, he's always been move-free when it comes to me."

Dierdre opened Meena's perpetually unlocked door. "Oh, he wanted to make a move, he was just being a gentleman. You know he double-checked to make sure the door was shut tight before leaving."

Meena went into the apartment, heading for Deven's room. "Maybe he was trying to follow me in." She didn't like that idea at all—if he wanted to come up, she would much rather that a guy be genuine about it rather than sneaky.

"Nope, he grabbed it and tugged before twisting and pushing to make sure it latched tight. Don't worry, I kept the sound turned off so you could have a private convo." She paused for a moment, her concern leaking through. "Are you going to see him again?"

"He's Deven's godfather. Of course I'll see him again." Meena laid her half-asleep son in the bed and tugged off his coat and shoes. Putting him in full sleepwear wasn't going to happen tonight, but at least she could make him comfortable.

"I'm glad you had a good time with him."

"I have a good feeling about him." When Meena turned toward the new voice, Vanna stood behind them in the doorway.

"Really? That's very comforting. Don't you need a questionnaire and two-hour interview to know these things?" Meena felt kind of snotty after she said it, but she didn't know how she felt about Kaleb right now, so the last thing she needed was pressure from her sisters about him. The fact that these two were on different sides of the issue—and Dierdre was concerned, no matter what she had said—just made it harder.

"Sometimes I just know. I'll need to actually meet and interrogate him for confirmation. Why didn't you invite him in to meet us all?"

"It was the wrong time. Another day. Maybe."

"How much does he know about all of this?" Vanna gestured to the well-worn interior, though Meena knew she actually meant the lotto they had won and their purchase of the building.

"Nothing as far as I could tell, though he did seem a little perplexed about the security and lack of other tenants. I told him that was a story for another day. I didn't want to spend our first real chance to talk discussing the winning ticket."

"He's definitely cute," Vanna said. "But then, Bennett did call him a hottie. Did she see him?"

"No, only pictures. You were watching for us to come back too?"

"No, I saw him when he arrived earlier. I just had the door open now so I heard you two talking when you came back up." She pointed between Meena and Dierdre.

Meena wanted to be annoyed that they were babying her, but she couldn't help being more amused than annoyed. It was nice having people who worried about her. "And the two of you were the only ones checking out my friend on the camera?"

"Of course not. Dierdre saved the first chunk of video from when he picked you up so the rest of us could check him out. We know you never date; we were curious."

"Like anyone in this building has any room to talk about me not dating."

"Hey, we're not talking about us right now." Diedre grinned.

Meena gestured them away from the door so she could come out of Deven's room and close the door behind her. "How were things here?"

"Quiet—so, utterly perfect in my opinion." Dierdre leaned one hip against the kitchen counter.

"We double-checked all the entrances after the last of the crew left to make sure it's all locked up for the night," Vanna said. "The storm is supposed to hit in a few hours. We may wake up to a layer of ice or snow."

"Or both." Meena reached for her favorite sleepytime tea. Not that she was ready to sleep quite yet, but it wouldn't hurt to get her ritual started a little early. "Either of you want a cup?"

"Nah, I better get back to my little one." Dierdre tapped the baby monitor attached to her hip. "Caelan hasn't been sleeping well lately."

"Change is hard for kids. I should make sure Karinda is ready for bed," Vanna said. "We'll talk tomorrow after we see if the older kids are going to school or not."

"Alright. See you both in the morning." Meena set her favorite mug next to the stove and filled the pot with water, setting it on the burner without turning it on yet. First, pajamas. It may have seemed ridiculous to get ready for bed so early, but she enjoyed a lengthy, restful bedtime ritual. Considering all the thoughts racing through her head, time to wind down was a necessity.

Chris had never understood her need to change into pajamas, enjoy her tea and some evening meditation, and journaling for a half-hour or more before bedtime. Unwinding from a busy day helped her fall asleep quickly and an early bedtime allowed her to start the morning with meditation and yoga.

She learned as a teenager that even a few minutes of morning meditation helped her start her day off on the right foot. Now that she had a little one who woke early in the morning, she needed an even earlier bedtime when she could swing it if she wanted to start each day off in blessed silence.

Evening meditation took a little longer than usual that night, so she was glad she had begun early. Spending time with Kaleb had thrown her for a loop and opened the door to the mental closet she had shoved her marriage into after Chris' death. Not dealing with her feelings and confusion had been so much easier than processing it all. Unhealthy, maybe, but that hadn't stopped her from being a productive member of society.

The herbal tea soothed her and she scribbled in her journal, letting it all flow onto the page. Maybe after a good night's sleep she would be able to make heads or tails of her feelings.

## Seven

WORKMEN FILLED THE main floor. The framers were finally bringing the shell of the building back to some semblance of usable space—in this case, the store front that the women would use to sell their crafts. Meena came to the bottom of the stairs thinking maybe she should be doing a few laps of the stairwell everyday along with her yoga.

Adam, the crew chief, stopped and looked over. "We're a little behind this morning because of the icy roads. Some of my guys aren't here yet," he apologized, as if she were counting heads and noticed that a couple were missing.

"No problem, I'm glad you could make it at all. I know most of the city is shut down still."

"We have a couple of guys coming from further away who will be in a little later when the roads clear."

"It's looking good. Andrea's been baking again

and asked me to bring down some sweets for you guys when you have a break." Meena passed over the nine-by-thirteen pan of cinnamon rolls. There was a second one in the communal room upstairs for the residents.

"It smells amazing. I'm sure everyone will enjoy them." He set the dish on a makeshift table in the corner of the room that also held the big orange water cooler.

Meena took a stroll through the space. It had been nothing but bare brick a week or so earlier. The men had framed out the walls and were now separating Andrea's studio from the rest of the retail area. She could hardly believe this was all coming together.

"We've only been working for a couple days," Mikey, a spiky-haired twenty-something member of the crew, came to stand beside her.

"I know, but I can already see how it's going to look in my head." Meena knew where every display case would be, how the various hand-crafted items would be set up and where the recessed lights would highlight certain areas. They had a detailed map tacked to the common room wall upstairs. It could always change, but a plan made it seem all the more real.

"I bet you're excited."

"We all are." She grinned and let out a breath of

happiness. "Well, I'll let you get back to work." She waved to them and headed back up the front stairwell, which ran from the main floor all the way to the roof of the building. The old pipe railing was rickety and corroded in several places and had only gotten a conditional pass from the safety inspector. Good thing Sheila was making a new one.

She came to the second floor, locking the door behind her so their hallway would be secure, and heard kids playing in the common room right away. School had been canceled thanks to the icy roads, so even though they were almost directly across the street from the elementary school, everyone was home today.

"How's it coming?" Dierdre asked.

"Progress. I bet the main floor will be all framed by the end of next week."

"I'll have to pop down to see it later today." Dierdre was acting as the contractor for the project, keeping everyone on their toes. She was a master when it came to the details.

"So, what are everyone's needs today? We can put together a schedule so we can take turns working," Andrea said as the others joined them in the hall. Everyone's doors were wide open, as they most often were, and the kids played together happily—for now, anyway.

"I need to do two big batches of soap. Two or three hours to mix and pour and then I'll be free for the rest of the day. I could start work on my taxes, if there's time," Deirdre said.

"I have a shoot this afternoon," Andrea told them. "One o'clock at the client's house—it will probably take an hour, and then I'll have some touch-ups to do. Good thing they only live a couple of blocks away. I'm hoping the roads are more than passable by then."

Everyone else chimed in with the things they needed to do for their businesses and Sheila plotted it all out on the white board they had posted in the hall so there would be two women available to ride herd on the kids at all times. Communal parenting had lightened everyone's loads, and being secure on this floor eased everyone's stress. Since they had won the lotto, there had been concern that someone might decide one of the kids was the path to an easy payout. Added to that, the limited info Bennett and Sheila had given on their crazy exes and the generic statements Dierdre had made about her apparently bad-news past life, and they had felt pushed to find somewhere they could make secure and feel safe in.

"First shift goes to you," Sheila said, gesturing to Andrea and Bennett. The rest of them retreated to their apartments or office spaces to take care of their business interests.

Meena left the door ajar to the apartment reserved for her jewelry-making business. Deven played well with the other kids and she totally trusted Bennett and Andrea, but it didn't hurt to keep one ear open for trouble. One never knew when the one of the boys would turn into a grumpy pants and start all three of them on a crying jag.

She walked over to the kitchen counter where she had left out the tools for the project she had started the previous day. One of the cabochons she had picked up in Leavenworth sat with the sterling silver bits she had already cut and prepped for assembly today. After setting an alarm on her phone, she got out the safety goggles, apron, and other paraphernalia she would need to put this pendant together and got to work.

She picked out some bezel wire that was the right height for her stone, cut it to length and trimmed it with her jig so the edges would marry right. She loved the feel of the fine file as it smoothed out rough edges and made perfect angles. When everything else in her life felt out of control, here, in her studio, she could control almost all of the variables and make things come together the way they should.

Once she was ready to start soldering, she popped

the window open and turned on the ventilation fan, and then spread some flux on the edges she was going to solder.

She worked meticulously through the steps of creating the circle, then attaching it to the silver backing plate and trimming the plate to the right width, leaving a little of the plate at the top, which she punctured and put a ring through.

Meena's mind barely registered the first ding on her phone that signaled an incoming text message. Dismissing it, she focused on bending the edge of the silver around the lapis lazuli stone so it wouldn't come loose and finished off the pendant.

There was another ding and a moment later the alarm she had set went off. "Well, that was good timing."

Where had the time gone? She was playing with the kids during the middle shift, so she cleaned up the detritus of her morning's work and put away her tools, then left the apartment, locking it behind her. She wasn't concerned about outsiders getting in to her things, but they had seven curious children and she didn't want to take the risk that one of them would wonder how her torch worked.

As she walked down to see how everyone was doing, she checked her text messages and found one. The first was Kaleb:

**I had a great time last night. When can we get back together?**

She grinned and typed back: **Come for dinner Saturday night. 6:00. My friends want to meet you.**

Kaleb: **Should I be scared?**

Meena: **Oh yeah. But don't worry, they've all had their shots.**

She laughed when he responded with two exclamation points.

Kaleb: **I'll be there.**

Now she was committed, even if she got cold feet later. She grabbed the red dry-erase marker that was for her and Deven and added a note on their communal white-board calendar.

"Wait, you're having dinner with the hottie?" Bennett asked as she saw what Meena was writing. "Are the rest of us invited?"

Meena turned to see Bennett's shirt today said "Breakfast, It's What's For Dinner." This made her smile, since that was true more often than not if Bennett was cooking. "I figured you would all want to meet him, but I'd rather you didn't totally overwhelm him before we even get through dinner."

Bennett threw an arm around Meena's shoulder. "If he can't handle us, then he can't handle you, because we all come as a package."

66

Meena laughed. "I know, but we should probably lull him into a sense of complacency first."

"If you insist. You can have him for dinner. But we'll have dessert together in there." She pointed to the room where the toddlers were gathered around a movie, the school-aged kids were working on crafts around one of the tables.

"Fine. Just try to act like you're sort of normal."

"No promises."

"I'm here to take over if you need to get some work done."

"Great. I'm going to start prepping my business taxes—Dierdre isn't the only one stressing over them. I didn't make enough to have to file for the business a year ago, so this is all new to me."

"Tell me about it. Tony said he could work them into his schedule, so at least we'll have someone competent making sure the forms are filled out once we have everything together."

"Now there's a hottie," Vanna said, joining them.

"You should go after that one," Bennett said with a touch of attitude. "You're all about the love and smoochies."

"I'll think about it. In the meantime, I'm also on duty this shift. Where's Andrea?"

They traded places and Meena joined the kids at the table, overseeing the paper and glue projects. She loved these kids and was thrilled to have them all in her life. The women had frequently traded babysitting over the past two years to facilitate jobs and as they started up their businesses, but not having to work off-site anymore had allowed her to spend more time with Deven and the other kids, as well as time to think and breathe without being exhausted already from a long day of work.

Everyone took a break for lunch, which went off with only a few hiccups, and then around two o'clock the third shift came in and Meena returned to her work. It wasn't always the most convenient way to run a business, but since finding these ladies, she felt more secure than she had in years. There wasn't anything she wouldn't do for them.

That evening Meena prepared dinner for Deven and herself, enjoying the time with just him as he messily colored a picture on the counter beside her. Pulling out her phone, she took a moment to check her email for any new orders. She froze when she started to read an email from a sender she unfortunately recognized.

**Your beauty and grace**
**Entice all of my senses**
**To love more surely**

## UNSHAKABLE LOVE

**When I can't see you
My day becomes dark and cold
Without your sunshine**

**Someday you and I
Will be one flesh together
For always my own**

Her flesh crawled. This was not the first time this guy had sent creepily personal poetry in her inbox and not signed it, insinuating that she had a relationship with him. This was another reason she wanted to live somewhere secure—the last thing she wanted was to let this crazy person anywhere near herself, her son, or her sisters.

She knew she would have to tell the other women about it. Up until now she had told herself that it was some joke, or it would stop if she didn't respond—she had tried asking him not to write anymore, but that hadn't helped at all. Maybe this *was* someone's sick idea of a joke, but the guy wasn't stopping. They deserved to know what was going on so they could be prepared in case he decided to do more than send emails. First, she had to get them alone—without all the kids. Maybe after the kids went to bed.

"Momma, when is dinner?" Deven asked. "I want to play with Bobby."

"You had a lot of fun playing with him today," she said. "We'll eat soon." She didn't bother to address going to play with Bobby; it wouldn't happen tonight. She picked up her phone and sent a group message before she chickened out and put it off—again.

**Meeting tonight once the kids are down. We need to talk.**

She pushed send and stirred the veggies in the pan again. Deciding they were fully cooked, she added them to the piles of rice on each of the plates she had already started for herself and Deven, and then carried them to the table. She set the phone on the table beside her and saw as the others chimed in that they would be there, one by one. All right. Time to focus on Deven's bedtime ritual, and then she could prepare for her meeting. The others were going to be freaked out and angry that she hadn't told them about it sooner.

Nothing she could do about it now.

# Eight

"WHAT'S UP?" ANDREA ASKED Meena when the women were finally all seated around the table, each carrying a baby monitor from their individual apartments despite the fact that their doors were all wide open.

Meena rolled the pages she had brought from her printer, needing something to do with her hands. "I've been getting some weird emails lately."

"We all have," Vanna said. "Ever since the lotto announcement with our faces on it."

"Wait, what kind of weird emails?" Dierdre asked.

In response, Meena passed around the slightly curled copies of the emails to everyone. "I get about one per week, or have for over a month. Number six arrived tonight. Maybe it's nothing. Maybe it's supposed to be a joke. But I can't help feeling it's something more."

"This is creepy." Dierdre read a page with a couple of messages.

"He talks like he thinks you're going to be together." Andrea pursed her lips and pushed the page to Sheila.

Meena nodded. "Yeah, it's disturbing. I was hoping he would stop on his own, but I realized today that this isn't just potentially going to affect me, but possibly all of you too. Especially now that we're the only ones living here."

"You should have told us sooner." Sheila shot her a dirty look.

"I know. I kept hoping it wouldn't be a big deal. This is different than the other stuff we've been getting, but not *that* different."

"Um, yeah, it is. He didn't sign it. He writes in freaking poetry for the woman he loves. He's delusional. This guy could be dangerous." Bennett passed the pages she had been looking at on down the line. "We need to do something about this."

"Unless you know how to track emails, I think we're at an impasse. Look, we're in a secure building with a good surveillance system thanks to Dierdre. We're all careful. I don't think there's much more we can do besides continuing to be vigilant. Mostly I just wanted you all to know."

"I bet your Army man knows someone who could

track down information from an email," Dierdre said. "If he doesn't know how to do that himself."

"I'm not bringing him into this."

"Why not, if he's Deven's godfather, then he probably feels some responsibility for making sure you're both safe, and he doesn't want to raise the boy himself, right, so protecting you will ensure a long, happy life."

"No. We're not bringing him into this." Meena wasn't ready to trust him with that much.

"Not yet?" Bennett asked.

"More likely never. He has a life outside of Deven and me."

"Until he decides that he doesn't want it to stay separate." Vanna couldn't have worse timing.

"Don't even go there, Miss Matchmaker." Was the room closing in on her, or was that just her imagination?

"Can I help it if I see wedding bells everywhere I turn?"

"Maybe you need to focus on bells for you and leave the rest of us out of it."

"You're the only one who currently has any prospects. Now, back to the topic at hand—Dierdre has done awesome things with the system, but that's not enough. We should contact the police." Sheila brought the conversation back to the main topic at hand.

"And tell them what? Some creep has sent me some letters but they aren't overtly threatening, and we have no clue who he is?"

"She's right," Andrea piped up. "The police here don't exactly have the best track record."

"Hey!" Sheila protested.

"I know, your sister-in-law and a few of her friends are great, but they aren't the detectives, and the police chief has been useless—they didn't listen to a word I said about Jared's murder and acted more like they were trying to cover it up than like they were investigating."

"Granted, your husband's case has been thoroughly mishandled, but maybe Lisa could suggest an avenue to pursue." Sheila looked like she was trying not to resent the dig on the police department, as if it were a personal affront against her sister-in-law. "If nothing else at least there will be a paper trail in case he steps things up. Without that, their hands will be tied even if they *want* to do something."

Meena debated for a couple of seconds, then decided she might as well explore her options—she really would like to stop these emails. "Fine, ask Lisa if she has any suggestions and we'll go from there. In the meantime, be extra watchful. This guy could be almost anyone. I honestly have no clue who he is."

"Um, not to cause problems, but could it be Kaleb?" Bennett suggested.

"No way." It was a gut reaction rather than a thoughtful one, but still, no way.

"He arrived in town about the time the emails started coming—Maybe he came when he said he did, and maybe he came earlier. And even if they started before he arrived, they're emails, he could have started sending them from *anywhere*. You ran into him by *accident* and he's doing his best to slide right into your life. Maybe he heard about the money and arranged for this transfer."

Meena shook her head. Not Kaleb. Surely. No matter what else he'd done, he wouldn't do *this*. "You clearly don't understand how the military works."

Dierdre took up Bennett's point. "Are you sure he's really working on base? I mean, you saw him with his friends, but could this have been all an elaborate setup to get to you?"

"Of course not." But if Meena was going to be completely honest with herself, could she really be sure of that?

There was a moment of silence.

"Not an ounce of doubt?" Dierdre asked.

Could she be sure? Was there any way to be certain he really had no clue about the lottery winnings, or that he wasn't behind it all? Maybe it was too soon to let him into her home, into her life. She had thought she'd known him before, but then he'd pulled away, distancing himself from her for no reason that she could tell as her relationship with Chris had strengthened. As Chris' best friend, he should have been around more, not less as time went on.

"I could tug on some lines and see what pops about him," Dierdre said. "I might also know someone who could track the IP address these are coming from and at least determine if they all came from this area. I'll check and get back to you in a day or two."

"In the meantime, I hate to say it, but you should reconsider letting him into the building. We should be *sure* that it's safe having him here before he comes inside," Bennett said.

Meena's head hurt a little, and her heart hurt a lot at the thought, but she nodded. They were right. She couldn't take any risks with her sisters or the kids. "Okay. I'll put him off." She hated to do that, especially when she was *almost* completely sure that it could not be him.

But what if she was wrong? Could she risk letting him in if he wasn't who she believed him to be? After all, he was Chris' friend, and she knew how that had turned out.

Meena: **Tomorrow night won't work after all, can I get a rain check?**

Kaleb stared at the message on his phone and frowned. **Of course. Is everything okay?**

She didn't respond immediately, but then he had missed the message when it first came through nearly an hour ago while he'd been in a meeting. He stuffed the phone back in his pocket and returned to his desk to work. Hopefully she would respond soon.

It was almost lunchtime when she wrote back that all was fine, she just needed to push off the dinner. But she didn't suggest another night.

She had no reason to lie to him, so why did he feel unsettled? Everything had seemed fine when they talked last.

He ran into Nash Peters as he entered the mess hall.

"How's life in Foreign Military Studies?" Nash asked.

"Fine, about the usual. Anything exciting going on over at the jail?"

"About the same as usual. Ethan and I were talking about going to see the new action flick tomorrow night. Want to join us? Or are you seeing your Indian beauty again?"

77

"Thought I was, but apparently I'm free. Sounds good." At least he wouldn't have to sit in his tiny apartment and stew.

It sounded far less interesting than dinner with Meena. Maybe he should send her some flowers. Would that seem pushy?

Maybe a small bouquet of lilies would hit the right note.

Meena couldn't sit at home wondering if she had made a mistake canceling her plans with Kaleb—especially after a big arrangement of mixed-color Peruvian lilies arrived at her door. Dierdre had compared the IP address on each of the emails and one she sent to Meena from their own system and figured that the emails had all been sent locally over the past weeks. Sheila's sister-in-law was tapping a friend on base to make sure that Kaleb was actually working on base and if he could have been in the area for that long.

Once she had the answer, Meena could reschedule their dinner, but until then, she'd have to wait. He had written her a couple of times since she had canceled their date the previous morning, and she had been forced into vagueness. She really hated that. Did he think she was blowing him off?

So, instead of staying home and staring at her kitchen sink, or going down to check out the construction updates for the second time that day, she decided a movie was in order. There was a new children's cartoon just the right age for Deven. The characters were all animals who got up to insane high jinks, so he clapped and laughed his way through the show. As they got up to leave, she wished she had invited Bennett and her daughter to join them—Grace would have enjoyed the movie as much as Deven had, despite the difference in their ages.

"Dat was good. I want to watch again," Deven said as they left the theater. He had his buttery little hand in hers and she wished she had pulled out the wipes to clean it up before they had gotten out of their seats.

"Maybe we'll have to buy it later." The show had been surprisingly intelligent, something she had enjoyed on an adult level as much as he had enjoyed on his level.

As they turned the corner into the main hall that led back to the door, she was surprised to hear Deven call out, "Kabe!"

Meena followed his gaze to Kaleb, who had stopped on his way into a theater across the hall. He looked over and found her. His brows lifted and he said something to the two guys beside him—one of whom he had been with when she'd run into him the previous week. All three were dressed down in street clothes.

The other two men eyed her, but then went into the theater, taking the huge tub of popcorn Kaleb had been holding. Kaleb, however, moved in her direction.

Crud. Just what she didn't need.

It took him a moment to make his way through the crowds of people crossing in the halls. "Did your thing get canceled, or did you give me the brush off to go to the movies with my man Deven?" Seeing Deven reaching for him, Kaleb swung the boy up into his arms.

"Hi, Kabe. We went to a movie." His greasy hand landed on Kaleb's face, but the man didn't seem to mind.

"Yeah, was it good? What did you see?"

Realizing they wouldn't be going anywhere right away, Meena dug into her bag to look for a wipe. "Sorry, he's all greasy." She pulled one out and wiped Deven's hands, then the shiny spot on Kaleb's cheek. "I'm sorry."

"It's fine. I don't mind."

He and Deven spent a couple of minutes talking about the show before Kaleb was able to shift his gaze back to Meena, who had tucked away the wipe. He didn't say anything, but his expression clearly asked, "So what gives?"

Feeling uncomfortable, she tried not to squirm under his look. "Like you said. There was a cancellation." Her canceling dinner with him, but that was beside the point.

"That seems to be happening to you a lot."

"Sometimes. How are things going?" She really wanted to explain everything. He looked hurt, confused and unbelievably handsome. How had she ever let Chris' good looks and charm convince her he was worth her attention when his friend was sitting right next to him?

Okay, that train of thought had to end right now.

"Well enough. I mean, there's no one nearly as pretty as you on base, but work is going fine."

She felt her face heat, though she rarely colored enough for others to tell she was blushing. He wasn't helping her out with comments like that. "Okay, your show is probably starting soon, so we'll let you get to it."

He reached out and took her hand. "I'd rather spend the time with you and Deven." His voice had softened and his expression reiterated his words.

"I need to get him to bed, but another time. I'm sure your friends will be wondering what happened to you."

81

He smiled and chuckled. "No, if I didn't show up, they'd figure it out pretty fast. But as you say, it's time to get him to bed. I really do want to get to know my godson better, and I want to make sure that I can help you out with anything you might need." He set Deven back on the floor.

"Thanks, I'll keep that in mind. Goodnight." Meena snagged her son's hand and gave Kaleb a little wave with the other.

When she got home, she was definitely going to check with Sheila to see if she'd heard anything. Having to put Kaleb off was unbearable.

# Nine

IT WAS MID-DAY ON Tuesday before Sheila came to Meena's door with her phone in hand. "Lisa called back with a report."

"Great!" She took the offered phone. "Hello?"

"Hi, Meena, I found out about that guy. Staff Sgt Kaleb Owen Muller. They said he's currently working in foreign military studies and that he just transferred on December ninth from Kandahar, Afghanistan where he has been deployed for a couple of years. He was out of country when you started getting those emails, and only had a week to visit family in Texas in between. He has no criminal record or infractions that give me the slightest concern."

Relief poured through her. Kaleb was definitely *not* her freaky emailer. "That is such great news. Thank you so much for looking into that for me."

"No problem. I'd really like to come in and take

a report about your creepy letters, so we have something on file in case this guy escalates, or you figure out who he is. There's not much else we can do about it right now, but having a record is the first step."

"Okay, great. When can you come over?"

They set up a time for later in the day and ended the call. She let out a squeal of happiness.

"Do I take it that your guy is in the clear?" Sheila asked.

"Yes. You have no idea how glad I am to be able to trust Kaleb."

"You *do* like him! I knew it wasn't just about him being Deven's godfather."

"No, it's not like that." Except that she was starting to wonder if it was.

"Right, whatever you say. I'm not saying that you should fling yourself headlong into a relationship— heaven knows that never worked out for me and I don't want you to get hurt. I'm just sayin', I thought you liked him more than you were admitting. I'm heading back to my drawing board. I put in the changes everyone suggested and I think I'm ready to finalize the design for the stair railing and draw it out on my table."

"Great. I can't wait to see it."

Sheila hadn't totally disappeared through the open door when she pulled out her cell phone.

Meena: **Hi, I wondered about rescheduling that dinner. Any night this week works for me.**

She waited for a few minutes, anxiously wondering if he would decide that she was too much work. But then her phone beeped.

Kaleb: **I'm open any evening in the next few days.**

Knowing the other women would want to meet and vet him, she went out to check the board. Everyone should be home the next night. **Okay, how about tomorrow night then? Do you still like spicy Indian food?**

Kaleb: **So much. Tomorrow is perfect. Is six still okay?**

Meena: **Yes. See you then!**

Okay, so she had a second...date? Outing? Except they weren't going out, they were staying in. Inning? She didn't know what to call it, but it was back on. She was going to make the best Chicken Tikka Masala he had ever eaten.

She wasn't sure if she was so excited because she was relieved that he wasn't her stalker, or if she liked him more than she had been letting herself admit, but she headed to her apartment with a new bounce in her step.

"Hey, Sergeant Muller," one of the office guys called to Kaleb the next afternoon when he was in the mess hall. "What *have* you been up to?"

The way he asked made Kaleb curious—it seemed strange that he would ask so pointedly. "Um, my work. Why?"

"One of the police officers over in Crystal Creek called yesterday and was asking questions about you: when you got here, where you were before, if you'd been in any trouble, etc. So, what have you been doing? The officer said she was just eliminating you from something, and seemed relieved when she learned when you arrived."

"I seriously have no clue. I mean, I know a woman over there, but that has nothing to do with, well, anything that the police might want me for." Unless Meena was under investigation or something. "When did the officer call you?"

"She had left a message with me last Friday, but she finally caught me at my desk right after lunch yesterday."

And Meena had texted to reschedule their dinner a little later? That couldn't be a coincidence. "So weird. Thanks for the heads up. I promise, I haven't done anything that would make the cops interested in me."

Six hours until he saw Meena again and could ask

her if she knew anything about the situation. He didn't want to have this conversation over the phone. She hadn't been particularly good at hiding her feelings in the past, but maybe she had learned a thing or two since?

He would definitely be paying close attention when he got to her place that evening. Something about the whole setup seemed hinky.

# Ten

WHY WAS SHE SO NERVOUS? It seemed stupid to be so wound up over dinner with Kaleb when she had eaten with him and Chris so many times in the past. She was more anxious about tonight than she had been the previous week when they had gotten together for dinner.

"That smells amazing," Bennett said, walking through the open door. "I miss Chicken Tikka Masala nights."

"That's why I made enough for you and Grace as well."

"Really? You're the best! Andrea has one of those pudding cakes ready to pop in the oven, so it'll come out gooey and fudgy when you finish eating. I can hardly wait."

"He'll die over that. He's a huge chocolate lover." At least she remembered some things.

"Good." Bennett looked her up and down. "Are you wearing that?" A hilarious question from someone wearing an "Accio Coffee" tee and sweat pants.

Meena looked at her tee and jeans. "Why not?"

"Seriously?" She didn't wait for an answer, just disappeared into the bedroom to rummage through the closet.

Amused, Meena added a few more shakes of the masala seasoning, stirred it in, and turned the heat down when she heard Bennett's call of "Ah-ha!" from the other room.

She went in and found a goldenrod-colored blouse laid out on the bed, paired with several pieces of gold jewelry from Meena's collection.

Bennett turned and looked her over again. "Those jeans are fine, but change your top and add some accents. Also, different shoes."

The outfit was more like what Meena would normally wear out in public, the top more caftan-like and flowy, the jewelry complimented her coloring more than the much simpler silver pieces she wore on days when she was working in her studio.

Bennett added some great purple flats that complemented the top and the purple stones in the necklace. "There you go." She checked her watch. "You have just enough time to change and touch up your makeup before he arrives. I'll keep an eye on dinner and set the table. I'll also keep an eye on Deven." She ducked out again without giving Meena a chance to protest.

"Apparently I'm changing clothes." Meena had intended to switch clothes originally, but she'd been sucked into her work that afternoon and hadn't emerged early enough to make dinner *and* find something appropriate to wear.

By the time she came out of the room, appropriately attired, Bennett was dishing up two plates of the meal for herself and Grace, who both liked spicy food.

"You weren't kidding about making plenty. You planning on leftovers for lunch and dinner for the next two days?"

"I wasn't sure how much he would eat. It's been a while since I cooked for a man."

"I'm sure you won't run out. You look perfect, by the way. I love your makeup like that. Exotic without looking overdone."

"Thanks. The table looks great." Bennett had never been one for a fancy table when they first met, but living together for the past couple of years, she had picked up a few skills from Meena—and imparted a few of her own along the way.

The buzzer rang, signaling that there was someone at the outside door.

Meena tapped the mouse on her laptop and the screen saver disappeared, showing Kaleb on the monitor downstairs holding what looked like a bottle of wine—he must have forgotten that she didn't drink, even though she appreciated the gesture. Did that mean he thought of this as a date? "I guess I'm up." She pushed the mic button. "I'll be right down."

She glanced around the room again, glad to see Deven was still engrossed in his movie, which was almost over.

"Have fun. Be careful. See you in a little over an hour." Bennett waived her downstairs.

Meena tried to calm her rapid heart rate as she took the stairs to the main floor, pushing the elevator button when she reached the bottom so it would be ready to go up in. The doors opened immediately.

When she opened the outside door, she had to catch her breath. Man alive, she loved the way his blond hair curled slightly, even though it was cut short.

"Hi." She stepped back out of the way for him to enter.

"Hi. I'm told this is a good vintage and would complement your meal." He tipped the bottle of sparkling white grape juice so she could read the label. "I noticed Deven likes soda, I wondered what he would think of this."

Meena was relieved, and even more appreciative of his thoughtfulness. "He'll probably love it. Sugar plus carbonation always equals fun as far as he's concerned."

"Great."

They crossed to the elevator and she pushed the button again so they could get inside.

"This looks like a pretty new elevator," he said,

"It is. The stairs have been redone as well, but don't let it fool you, the floor we're going to is still in desperate need of an update."

The doors opened a few seconds later, showing the dingy off-white walls and doors with the worn brown carpeting.

"You weren't kidding," he said after taking it all in. "What happened to everyone else who lived on this floor?"

"There hasn't been anyone else for a long, long time. I'll tell you about it later. This is my place." She turned into her apartment, which was painted in gold and jewel tones. Deven was parked in front of the movie—which he'd seen a dozen times already, but still watched raptly, and Bennett was nowhere to be seen. She had lit the candles on the table before leaving and Meena wished she could put them out without making an issue over them. She hadn't intended to turn this into a date-date.

"Nice, you've obviously done some painting in here," he looked around.

"We all did in our apartments. We've lived in boring rooms for too long before we moved here. We talked about doing the halls, but haven't gotten around to it. When we move upstairs in the fall, they'll just be gutting this floor anyway."

"When did you move in?"

"Only a few days before I ran into you, actually."

He paused in front of the stained-glass looking painting that Comfrey had made for her, and that she'd hung over the sofa. "Unshakable?" he asked, reading the word on it.

"Comfrey, she's one of the ladies who teaches the classes that we sometimes attend. Anyway, she talked to us about picking a power word, something that described what we wanted to be more than anything, and then she painted these pictures for us. We each have one with our own power word."

"That's pretty cool."

"We think so."

Credits started to roll on the movie and Meena flipped off the TV with a remote. Deven turned their way as if being released from a spell. "Kabe!" He hopped up and ran over.

"Hey, buddy. How are you doing?" Kaleb scooped the boy into a quick hug and listened to him prattle while Meena poured glasses of ice water and two flutes for the sparkling juice.

The guys came to the table as she set the bowls of vegetables, rice, and the chicken and sauce on the table runner.

They had dished up dinner and she had just put a bit of chicken into her mouth when he lowered the boom.

"So, was it you who had me investigated, or one of the other ladies here?"

Meena choked on the food, but managed to chew and swallow rather than spewing it across the room. "What?"

"It was one of you, wasn't it, who had the cops check up on me?" He very casually started eating his meal, as if they were doing nothing more than discussing the weather.

"Um, okay. Yeah." Did she brush it off as over-protectiveness or explain part of it? If she explained part, he would want to know all. Would he feel that he had to do something about the weird letters if she told him, or be offended that she had him checked?

He set down his fork and met her gaze, hurt and confusion in his eyes. "Did you think I'm a liar? What were you looking for?"

So much for the pleasant meal. Though he was being perfectly reasonable, she still worried. Bennett's husband had apparently acted perfectly reasonable before striking out at her. Was Kaleb secretly like him? Bennett hadn't recognized the signs of an abuser from her ex until after they were married. "Look, I honestly believed you, but there have been things going on, since before you came back from Afghanistan, actually, and I had to be absolutely sure that you didn't have any connection to them. The timing of running into you was kind of pushing the limit of coincidence. I wanted to believe it wasn't you, but I had to really *know*. And part of our deal here is that we don't bring men into our home without a clear background check. Even the workmen have to be screened—which has been a major pain."

When he didn't say anything, she continued, desperately wanting him to understand, if it was even possible. "I know that it seemed like I was blowing you off the past several days, but I had to wait for confirmation. You have to understand. You have to wait for intel for your job before making a move sometimes."

"This isn't war."

"No, but some of these ladies have been through war."

"More, Mama!" Deven said, holding out his sippy cup.

"I thought it was just a normal shelter—you

95

weren't battered, were you? I mean, I realize that I don't know all of the details of what happened, but I didn't miss that much, did I?"

She took the cup and added a little more sparkling cider while she answered. "No, you didn't. There is only the one shelter here in town. If you go into the surrounding towns, some have a battered women's shelter, but ours had a mix of reasons for why the women had come. Some had been abused, and some had other reasons for being there. We have to be careful."

Kaleb nodded and then picked up the naan bread that had been sitting on the edge of his plate. "I grabbed the chance to come to Leavenworth partly because you were in the area the last time I heard from you, and I was anxious to make sure that you were okay. Running into you in town—that was honestly a fluke. You know me, if I'd known how to reach you, I would have just contacted you instead of creating some coincidental meeting. What's going on here? Why is this place locked down like a fortress? I mean, security I get, especially if some of these ladies might still be in danger, but there are still a lot of unanswered questions rolling through my head."

And here came the explanations. She paused for a moment to consider, then decided to risk telling him about it. "I've been getting strange and slightly creepy emails since a couple of weeks before you arrived in town. And once, just before we moved here, I had a package left on my doorstep." She walked through the history with him and what her sisters had thought or said.

"I thought you knew me better than that." Disappointment clouded his eyes, but he didn't seem angry about her doubts, just sad.

He hadn't eaten much, but then again, neither had she. When Deven started chanting for seconds, Meena wondered if he had actually out-eaten them both. As she put more food on Deven's plate, she offered Kaleb the only explanation she had. "I thought I knew you once, but you pulled away the last few months before you and Chris deployed, and I had thought that I knew *him* before we married, but I don't think that's true anymore. Did you know he cheated on me when you were deployed?"

His face closed off and his gaze slid sideways.

She nodded. "So you did. And you said nothing." That was a bitter realization, even though she had known that he was really Chris' friend first and last.

Kaleb lifted a hand, asking for a chance to talk. "Apparently it had been going on for a while, but he knew I would be livid, so he didn't tell me. I found out by accident the day before he died. I threatened to tell you if he didn't, but then after he died, I didn't

97

think that knowing would make life easier for you, so I kept it to myself, and then you dropped off the face of the planet. How did you find out?"

"He emailed me, just before going on that last convoy." She wouldn't tell Kaleb that in that email Chris had practically bragged about his conquests since he'd left, and that there had been more than one woman. She had known their marriage was in trouble for some time, and regretted marrying him, but that had been the final straw. She had asked a friend about divorce attorneys the next day, though she hadn't called anyone before the news came through. And then she didn't need one after all. She had felt torn— grateful not to have to go through a messy divorce, sorrow over losing the man she loved, and guilt for the thought she'd had after receiving his email that she hoped he never came back—no matter how angry she had been, she hadn't wanted him dead.

That feeling of guilt still followed her.

"I'm so sorry. You didn't say anything."

"What good would it have done? His family would have blamed me if I told them. He was your best friend. Kaleb, I had *no one*. I had to cut ties with my family when I married him, and they didn't want me back with his baby—I even reached out to them eventually, but they refused to talk or write me back. His family practically shut me out after he was gone. I had *no one. Nothing.* I could have reached out to you, but you had effectively cut me off after Chris and I got serious. After all of that, I didn't know if I could trust you to be on my side."

He winced. "Which brings us full circle to why you had me investigated as a possible stalker. I guess I understand why you didn't think you could depend on me, though believe me when I say that backing off from our friendship was the only thing I could do at the time."

"I didn't think the stalker was you, but I didn't trust my own judgment. Not when everyone I thought I could trust had shut me out. Obviously, I'm not a very good judge of character."

"Mama! More juice!" Deven pushed his plastic cup to her and she poured a little more sparkling juice in it. She would have to cut him off soon—there was only so much sugar before bedtime if she didn't want him bouncing off the walls.

Several seconds passed before Kaleb spoke, his voice soft. "I'm sorry that I wasn't a better friend to you."

"Don't worry about it now." She lowered her eyes to her dinner and they ate in near silence for the next few minutes with only Deven and their responses to him puncturing the air.

Finally, he broke the silence. "I kept trying to find

you online, through Google searches, everything, and I couldn't find any references after the obituary."

She considered for a moment. "What name did you search?"

"Meena Bertrand. And Meena Sharma."

She chuckled. "Didn't you know Meena isn't my real name? I mean, I never, ever use my real name socially, but you had to have heard it a few times."

"What? Wait, oh my heck, I totally forgot that. I don't think I ever heard it except at your wedding. What is it again?"

"Mahendran. Mahendran Anik Sharma Bertrand: it's a ridiculous mouthful. I know, it's shocking that I would go with a nickname instead, right?"

"Um, yeah, shocking. Is Mahendran a common name for girls in India?"

"No. But Indra is the Hindu god of protection, and my parents felt like I would need extra protection growing up in this country with the way the world was going. So they named me after him. Not one of their kindest choices." Thankfully they had chosen more American-sounding Indian names for her younger sisters. She pushed back the regret at being cut out of their lives. Though she occasionally checked in on their Facebook feeds to see what they were up to, it was no substitute for an actual conversation.

When they stood from the table, Kaleb said, "I'd be happy to do dishes. That was a really great meal."

"I'll let you." She put away the leftovers and wiped everything down while he loaded the ancient dishwasher and scrubbed the pans and bowls.

"So, all of your friends here are also women from the shelter?" he asked after a few minutes.

"Yes. Bennett was there first, then Sheila and Dierdre before me. The other ladies came in over the next month or so while I was there, and we staggered as we left."

"Were you the only women there at the time?"

"No, unfortunately, there were quite a few others, but we didn't all bond with the others like the six of us did. Actually, I don't think anyone but Dierdre bonded with Vanna at first. Sheila and Andrea moved into an apartment together shortly after Vanna arrived. Bennet and I moved out the following month. Our friendships in the shelter strengthened as we attended training meetings, support groups, and helped each other with babysitting. Some people in town also provide extra training to help us gain life skills." Vanna had become a friend, but that hadn't been a strong connection for Meena until after they had won the lotto and they had started to work together more as a group.

"I'd like to meet all of these women who have supported you."

"You will." She glanced at the clock. "In a few minutes. Brace yourself—unless you want to cry off."

"Why would I want to do that?"

"You really have to ask after you were investigated?"

Kaleb studied her for a long moment. "There are some tangles in our past that we'll have to unravel, to work through, and I admit that I'm hurt that you didn't turn to me, or trust me, but I also understand why you didn't. Everyone you know and love has turned away from you. I'm here now and I want to be here, helping you. I want to help you figure out who's sending you the letters and put an end to it."

She wasn't sure if he was doing this out of guilt or something more. "Why?"

He paused a moment. "I'm Deven's godfather."

Right, that. "And you don't want to be responsible to raise him if something happens to me. Don't worry, one of my sisters would be happy to take on that job."

"That's not what I meant. I wasn't offering to protect you so I don't get stuck with responsibility."

"Really? What did you mean?" She met his gaze, silently begging for him to be honest and tell her, straight out, what was going through his head. Was he interested in her, or was he just trying to be a friend? And what did she want him to want? She wasn't even sure about that.

Apparently he wasn't a mind reader, because he shrugged one shoulder. "You and Deven matter to me. Not just because of Chris. I want to make sure you're going to be okay. I hope you'll let me help you."

There was honesty in his voice, but he hadn't indicated more than friendship, which was fine. She didn't need a man, so why did she feel let down? "Okay. I'm warning you, we can be a little chaotic when we all get together. Especially with all of the kids in the mix."

"Hey, you know about my family—I thrive in chaos."

With three married sisters, all of whom had kids, she didn't doubt it.

# Eleven

ALMOST EVERYONE WAS already in the communal area when Meena, Kaleb, and Deven joined them a few minutes later.

Andrea was the first to come over, ever the mom-type, she extended her hand for a shake. "I'm Andrea Rossi. I'm pleased to meet you, Sergeant."

"Same here."

She introduced everyone else, including the various children, and Dierdre and Caelan joined them just in time to get in on introductions.

"Come sit with us," Bennett said, nudging him toward a chair. "Meena tells us you're a chocolate fan."

"Anyone who doesn't like chocolate needs their head examined."

"I completely agree. You'll love Andrea's fudge pudding cake." When he sat, she turned to him in the way that some people misconstrued as flirty when Meena knew she was just easing them in for an interrogation. "So, tell me every tiny detail about yourself. Meena has been vague about how you met."

The girls at the far end of the table grumbled a little as they cleared away their Uno cards, but the promise of chocolate cake kept the grumbling to a minimum.

He looked over at Meena and grinned. "All right. Chris and I arranged to meet for dinner at this great little restaurant a few miles from base and we got lucky—Meena was our server. I arrived first and met her before he showed up. I checked for a ring, flirted lightly, wondered if she would actually go out with a customer who hit on her—it's a little cliché. Then Chris arrived and that was the end of that fantasy. After flirting outrageously with her all through dinner, he asked her out when she brought the check. Chris and I were best friends, so I couldn't exactly ask her out after he did, but I saw a lot of Meena while they dated."

Deven climbed onto Meena's lap and she had to resituate him to see Kaleb over the dark head. "Give me a break, that's not at all how it happened."

He turned to her with a look of challenge. "Really? What did I get wrong?"

"You didn't flirt with me. You were friendly, sure,

but you never paid any special attention to me. And so you know, I asked someone if I could switch tables so I could serve you—you weren't even seated in my area."

Kaleb stared at Meena as Andrea set a bowl of steaming chocolate pudding cake in front of him, topped with a huge scoop of vanilla ice cream. It barely registered. "That's not true."

"It most certainly is." This was definitely not the way she ever envisioned this topic coming up for discussion, but though she thought it ought to be more awkward admitting this in front of anyone, it took some of the pressure off of her that a private discussion would have caused. The fact that they were both treating the subject lightly helped.

"I flirted."

"Either you're not nearly as good at flirting as you think you are, or you did it in your mind because that, my friend, was not flirting." She accepted her own bowl of dessert, along with a small one for Deven, who she moved back to the booster seat between her and Kaleb.

"Huh." He looked a little dazed. "You were interested in *me*?"

"Do you think I'm blind?"

"Apparently he does. Or maybe just half blind," Bennett suggested.

"Seems like the best guys are always the ones who don't really put themselves out there," Dierdre added ice cream to a bowl for her daughter, Caelan.

"Are you going to eat that or just stare at it?" Andrea asked.

Still looking a little distracted, Kaleb lifted a spoonful of the dessert to his mouth and when he tasted it, his eyes widened. When he had finished savoring and swallowed, he asked, "Do you want to get married?"

Andrea laughed. "Sorry white boy, you're not the one for me. But I can get you the recipe. It's simple, even for non-bakers."

He let out a huge sigh of disappointment. "I guess I can settle for the recipe, if I have to."

"Did you look for our girl here when you got to Camp Leavenworth?" Dierdre asked. "You know, before you stumbled across her only a couple miles from base."

"I did, actually. I went back to her old apartment in Kansas City, but they had a new manager. She didn't know who Meena was, and didn't have the back records at the office. I asked a couple of the tenants, but they didn't have any idea of where she went. That was a few days before I ran into her in town."

Meena was surprised to hear he had gone to so

107

much work. He'd said he'd looked for her online, but tracking her down to an old apartment was another issue entirely.

"Do you know about the emails Meena's been getting?" Dierdre jumped right in.

"Yeah, she told me over dinner."

Now Meena was glad that the conversation had maneuvered over to that subject. Having to hear about it from Dierdre would probably not have made Kaleb happy.

"I like letters," Caelan said. "Miss Andrea sent me one when she visited Bobby's grandparents."

"That's cool. I like letters too. Miss Meena wrote really great ones. Chris always let me read them." Kaleb scooped up another huge bite of the dessert.

"Are you going to help us? Do you know someone who can track an IP address?" Dierdre asked.

"I do know someone who's a wiz on computers. Send me what you've got and I'll have him see what he can do."

She nodded, then eyed him speculatively. "You're a paratrooper, so you have special skills, right?"

Kaleb studied Dierdre warily. "We're not SEALs if that's what you mean, but we do have a few extra talents we've developed. What are you looking for?"

"Like how to break into buildings?"

His brows furrowed. "That's not something we're trained to do, but I know someone who's pretty good at it. Why?"

"Could you bring that friend to try to break into here? I need to know if we have any security holes that need to be filled in, anything I've missed, before anyone else figures out how to get through them."

"I'm sure he has a lot on his plate already," Meena said, worried that Dierdre was going to push Kaleb into doing something that would make him uncomfortable. This was getting out of hand quickly.

His shoulders relaxed. "We'd be happy to help. I'll get Ethan and Nash to come over on their next evening off and we'll see what we can do. Keeping Meena and Deven safe is a priority for me, and the guys are always happiest when they've been given a challenge."

"Good. Don't tell us when—just come see if you can evade the cameras and access the building somehow. If the police catch you, we'll cover you."

"You're sure you're not trying to get me arrested to keep me away from Meena?"

She chuckled. "Not a chance. She wouldn't let me even if that was what I wanted. I will, however, need information on your friends so we can clear them before they come over."

"Sounds good."

"And then come in for dessert afterward. I'll have ice cream in the freezer if nothing else." Andrea was never one to turn people away hungry.

"I'll definitely remember that. This stuff was amazing." He scraped up that last of the dessert in his bowl.

"Now that's out of the way, what do you look for in a woman or relationship?" Vanna rested her chin on one fist, studying him. She looked out of place in her business attire compared to the other women in their jeans and t-shirts, but she never acted like she even noticed.

"Um, what?" he fumbled.

Meena huffed. "You do *not* have to answer that question. Vanna's all about matchmaking, and if you tell her answers like that, she's bound to try to hook you up with someone."

Kaleb looked at Meena for a considering moment then turned to Vanna. "In that case, I want someone dependable, who's creative and able to make a home, but who also has interests of their own. I want kids, at least a couple. I've been deployed enough that I've learned the value of a home base, whether that's in the States, or in another country, somewhere that's a safe zone where I can decompress, find peace. I've been struggling with sleep lately, PTSD isn't much fun, so I need someone who understands if I need to get up and work out or go for a drive in the middle of the night. And who isn't going to think that it's a reflection on them or that I'm on the prowl for a new woman. I want someone who will trust me, and let me take care of them, while they also try to take care of me. I want a partner, someone who is committed to making it work and will call me out when I cross a line. She can't be weak willed or willing to take a back seat in our relationship, I want a partner."

Vanna nodded. "Huh. That's a pretty good list. You've been thinking about it."

"I have. I've been in the Army for almost fourteen years and I'd be happy to have a home."

"Good to know." Vanna scraped the bottom of her bowl, almost studiously avoiding Meena's gaze.

"Can't get much plainer than that," Bennett said, shooting a pointed look at Meena, who pretended not to understand it.

"Seconds?" Andrea asked everyone.

"Me!" half the kids called out.

"No," all the moms answered for themselves and their children.

"I'm pretty full from Meena's masala," Kaleb said.

Andrea put a hand on her hip. "She made you masala and didn't bring me any? I knew something smelled amazing down the hall. Maybe I was too hasty in serving her."

Meena just laughed. "Don't worry, there are plenty of leftovers. Come have some with me for lunch tomorrow."

"You're forgiven."

When they left the room twenty minutes later, the weirdness Meena felt about the very personal conversations had melted away and she was thankful that her friendship with Kaleb appeared to have survived the evening intact.

"Your apartment door is wide open. Hold on while I check it out," he said as they approached it. Apparently, he'd missed the fact that she'd left it open earlier.

Meena laughed. "We're the only ones in the building. We have an open-door policy—if the door is open, you're welcome to walk in and chat. If the door is closed, please knock first, or maybe even wait until later. Since we'll leave the door open while we run to one of the other apartments to talk to each other, we sometimes forget to close them. Other than Sheila's brother and his wife, I think you're the first person we've had on this floor since we moved here that wasn't actually hired to move or fix something."

"Huh. I hadn't thought about that. It's a good policy—the open-door thing. It establishes boundaries, but still keeps things casual most of the time between you. Don't you ever get annoyed or need a break from all of the community?"

"Yes, that's why we respect each other's privacy when the doors are closed." They walked past her place to the elevator, though their steps had slowed.

"This was an interesting experience," he said.

"This was about normal for our group."

"Heaven help me."

Meena laughed. "Well, you're committed now, buster. You have to put up with us."

"I'm okay with that. I'll have Ethan see what he can do on the computer side, and then we'll do our best to break in. I'll send you a message with Nash and Ethan's info so Dierdre can do her thing and I'll be waiting for the email with one of your letters to see what Ethan can do with it."

"I feel safer already." They came to a stop at the elevator. It was nearly time to put Deven in bed and Meena considered inviting Kaleb back to her apartment for tea or something, but she needed time to process everything that was going on.

"Dierdre's a big stickler on security—is there a reason for it? You know, besides your stalker? And what does your landlord think about it?"

They were ending things on a happy note—she didn't want to open a new can of worms and possible sour things between them. "And that gets back around to another long story, which we don't have time for tonight."

113

"You owe me the whole version one of these days."

"You'll get it one of these days."

"Good. Talk to you soon."

"Counting on it."

They stood, face to face for another long moment before he finally shifted back from her and pushed the elevator button.

It dinged as the doors opened and he backed into the elevator. The door shut and Meena turned to go back to her place.

Vanna stood in the hallway, her arms crossed over her chest. "Oh yeah, you two are *just friends*." She turned and walked away, shaking her head.

Meena let out a breath. Maybe Vanna was right—the evening had been rather fraught with confused feelings and impressions, but it definitely felt like something more than friendship several times. He had liked her before Chris had joined them. Maybe there was a chance for more than friendship after all.

# Twelve

COMING HOME NEVER used to seem so lonely. Kaleb probably should have been relieved that the evening was over and everything had ended on a good note—a miracle, really, considering how badly everything could have gone. Those had been some tough topics, and her friends, well, they didn't pull any punches.

He was okay with that—he preferred it to women who tried to be subtle and hint at what they wanted or wanted to know, especially since hints were usually lost on him.

Feeling tired despite the comparatively early hour, he slumped onto one of the lumpy chairs provided in his place on base. The place was pretty charmless—not like what Meena had done with her apartment. It would have helped if he had put up any kind of decorations, even pictures leaning on a table or something, but decorating had never been his thing. He had never felt like it was necessary or useful before.

His phone vibrated in his pocket, as it had done several times throughout the evening, but seeing his mom's and sisters' names pop up on the screen, he had put off reading the messages. No doubt it was pictures of kids or something that would keep.

To his surprise, there were no pictures of kids this time.

Mom: **Anyone heard from Kaleb lately? I can't reach him on the phone.**

Ellen: **You'd think we would hear from him more since he moved back to the states, not less.**

Cheryl: **That's a man for you.**

Mom: **Kaleb, when you read this, please drop us a note so we know you're alive.**

Kaleb shook his head and searched the emoticons until he found a couple of notes tied together with a line.

**Here are two.** And he posted the image.

Cheryl: **Very funny. Now, what have you been up to? Do you like the new base? Are you seeing anyone?**

That was a loaded question.

Kaleb: **I know I'm hilarious. I've been working, sleeping, eating, oh and I ran into Chris' wife. Their** son Deven's a hoot—I am, in fact his godfather, so I'll be keeping in touch.

Everyone asked how Meena was doing and commented on how glad they were that she was well and he'd found her. They chatted for nearly twenty minutes before they needed to get their kids in bed.

The apartment felt less tiny and sad after that, but only a little.

He flipped to his picture gallery on his phone and checked out some shots of Meena and Deven and realized that here was another reason that his world was brighter than it had been in a long while. He didn't love the apartment he was in, but he would think of it as a stepping stone, and everything would be fine.

"I found where your messages are originating from. Sort of," Ethan said as he came up to Kaleb's desk on Thursday afternoon.

Kaleb brightened "Really? Do we get to go intimidate someone now?"

"Sorry, I can only track them down to the area here. We would have to talk to the ISP to get more specific, but they won't do that without a really good reason. I'll work on a better solution."

"You're useless."

117

"Let me be useful instead. You said they asked us to break into the building?"

"Yep."

"Nash and I are free tonight. How about you?"

"Tonight it is. I'm thinking six-thirty—it's dark long before that. We can go after dinner and see what we can figure out. We'll need to case out the place before we can form a plan of attack."

"Sounds good."

Later that evening, the three of them stood on the sidewalk outside the building, far enough to be out of camera range, considering the options.

"No balconies," Nash said. "And the fire escapes are pretty far up there."

"Limited entrances," Ethan said.

"And they mostly have fancy locks: key cards, numbered pins, and cameras." Kaleb had been thinking over this since Dierdre asked him for help. On his way out on Wednesday he had even checked the door to the stairwell and found it locked the same way as the outside door. There was some serious paranoia going on, and he couldn't help thinking it was more than an abusive ex or Meena's stalker.

"Sounds like they've covered all the basics," Nash said.

"Let's go find some unbasics, then," Ethan suggested and led the trio around the building.

They circled the place, checking for extra cameras, working to stay out of their range, and came back to the beginning again.

"The windows all look new." Nash made some notes in his phone.

"They have good locks," Ethan said. "I recognize the company that made them. Could we access the building from the roof? I checked it on Google Earth today, there's a door up there."

"Who knows if it even opens anymore? We'd have to figure out how to get up there to begin with," Nash said.

"I could make that happen. How are your climbing skills?" Ethan asked.

"You mean hand over hand? It's six stories," Nash complained. "I mean, I'm the man, but it's *six stories*. No one could climb a rope that tall without one of their alarms going off. We'd need a launcher to even attempt it."

"Are you a wimp or what?" Ethan had a long and entertaining history of egging Nash on. "Besides, we could take the fire escape."

"But it doesn't go to the roof, so that's a second climb. It might be doable, though."

"After we scale the building, who's to say we could even get in the door?"

"You have a lock pick set."

119

"Unless there's a dead bolt," Kaleb added to their banter.

"Then you call your girlfriend and she lets us in from below. Or we repel down and try again a different way." Ethan was unfazed.

"We'd have to check out options, but I have an idea for a way in that we could try tonight." Nash grinned and headed around the building again, trudging along the edge of the community garden, now stiff and silent in the winter cold.

They came to the row of electric meters attached to the side of the building and he turned off all the ones that showed movement, indicating electricity usage.

The lights upstairs all turned off.

"Now what?" Ethan asked.

"Now we go back around to their main entrance and wait."

They huddled in the dark, just beyond the camera's reach for ten minutes. Fifteen. Twenty. Kaleb was starting to think this would be a bust when the door finally opened and Nash zipped onto the porch, grabbing the emerging woman around the chest to lock down her arms, while simultaneously sticking his foot in the door.

Bennett apparently saw him coming and managed to get one arm outside of Nash's grasp. Her fingers went into what passed for his hair and yanked hard while she simultaneously struck out at his kneecap behind her with one foot. He stumbled slightly and the door swung closed.

Undeterred, Nash tried to grab her free arm, swearing profusely as she wriggled and fought for dear life. A moment later he had her pressed between himself and the outside wall.

"Well, that didn't go as planned," he said, breathing heavily.

"Give me a second and I'll really kink your plan out of shape," Bennett hissed.

"Settle down." Kaleb decided it was time to step in. "Bennett, it's Kaleb. Remember how Dierdre asked me to bring some friends to try to break in? This big buffoon is Nash. Nash is going to let you go now. Try not to kill him."

Bennett turned her head toward Kaleb and narrowed her eyes. "I should have guessed you were behind the power outage. What was Dierdre thinking?"

Nash stepped back, pulling Bennett from the wall and then releasing her.

She turned and kicked him in the shins. "You were told to break in, not to molest one of us."

He rubbed his leg. "Ow, I'll try to keep that in mind next time. You're a hell cat."

"Thank you. Can you turn the power back on now?"

"No problem. Then we'll need to reconnoiter with you ladies. I'm Nash Peters, by the way." He offered her a hand.

She crossed her arms in front of herself, glaring. "Don't worry, I'm not likely to forget your name anytime soon."

He put on the cocky grin again and headed for the power meters, Ethan tagging along behind to help.

"I guess we failed that attempt," Kaleb said, hoping to lighten the mood.

Grudgingly she tugged her jacket closed over her "You Had Me At Bacon" tee. "You almost succeeded. If it had been Vanna, he would have won that tussle much easier and you'd be inside. Of course, you can't access the stairs or elevator without my code, but you would have been in the building."

The lights came back on to the windows upstairs and the guys returned.

"Come on in." Bennett used her key card and added a code, blocking their view of the keypad.

When they got to the second floor a moment later, the other ladies waited in the halls, and a couple of the kids looked like they'd been crying.

"Oh, man, I didn't mean to upset the kids," Nash said, honestly apologetic. "I'm sorry."

Dierdre's brows lifted. "I don't suppose someone trying to break in will worry too much about what the kids are going to do, other than if they might get in the way."

Nash rubbed his hand over the stubble of hair on his head. "Still, we'll keep them in mind next time and try not to upset anyone."

"Come sit down and tell us what happened. I have some cookies and milk." Andrea waved everyone toward the common room.

"Cookies!" Deven called out, then shot into Kaleb's open arms. "Kabe, we get cookies!"

Kaleb swung the kid up into his arms. "Yes, we do. Do you like them?"

"Yes!"

Everyone had their treats and then half the ladies put the kids to bed, or down for some quiet reading time while Dierdre, Bennett, and Meena sat down to talk to the three men.

"So, what did you find, besides the power meters?" Dierdre asked.

"It's pretty tight security. We didn't want to try forcing the front door, which is honestly the weakest point of entry on the ground."

"Why not?" Sheila asked.

"It's too early in the evening and more likely to be noticed by a neighbor or someone driving by. Plus, it would damage the door. That doesn't mean that it won't be used to access your apartments, but it's less ideal."

"We will soon have another keypad on the access to the stairwell in the front and there's a lock on the door to our floor. Since that stairwell goes all the way to the roof, we'll need an alternate egress option as well." Deirdre pulled up the floor plan on her computer and showed it to them. "It's fine while it's just the six of us, but once the rest of the building fills up, which could be awhile, it could potentially become an issue."

"Good point. We were wondering about roof access. Your average burglar isn't going to bother with it, but it's definitely possible to climb it with the right equipment, and there's always the chance of a helicopter drop onto the roof. Depending on the person's resources. What kind of resources does this hypothetical enemy have?"

"Endless. You know, hypothetically speaking." Dierdre didn't even blink at the suggestion, which make Kaleb wonder once again just who they were expecting to have show up.

"Right now the stairwell between the door to the roof and the sixth floor is non-existent, but they're going to put it back in when they frame up the sixth floor, so that's only a month or so away," Meena told them.

"Glad we didn't try accessing it up there yet, then. That would have been a rude awakening," Kaleb said.

"But at least it would have been your rude awakening and not mine." Bennett rubbed at her arm.

"Sorry about that, your ferocity caught me by surprise and I didn't manage the hold as well as usual," Nash apologized. "Plus I'm usually not so concerned about causing discomfort when I've grabbed someone like that."

She looked at him. "Lame excuse."

Dierdre made notes. "But that trick taught us that we need to expand the camera range around the door. And a generator for the security system needs to cover cameras as well as the entry pads."

"It'll need to cover the wifi router as well, otherwise we won't be able to see the images, even if the cameras are working," Meena added.

"I thought I had that covered, but apparently I didn't wire in something in that loop." Dierdre scribbled several more lines.

Ethan suggested a couple more pieces of equipment that left the other two women with confused expressions, though Dierdre seemed to understand what he was talking about.

"Are you going to try again?" Dierdre asked.

"I would have to borrow some equipment to try a roof approach, but if there's no way to get from the roof to the sixth floor..." Nash said. "It would be easier to use the fire escape to cover most of the floors with only a little climbing from the top of it to the roof."

"Try it without the fire escape," Bennett challenged. "We won't change a thing. I'd like to see if you can find a way around the problems."

Nash stared her down. "Oh, we can do that."

"Good. I dare you."

"Now she's playing rough. A dare from Bennett is serious," Meena said.

"And Nash never backs down from a dare. Which is why he's had so many broken bones," Ethan said. "And you can't *borrow* equipment from base."

"I know someone who has a few items. Off base. Legally acquired, he says. I think I could sweet talk him into lending them to us if we refill the bottle."

"In that case, I guess we'll be back," Kaleb said. He gave all three of the women a hard stare. "Are you sure the building owner isn't going to mind?"

"I guarantee it." Dierdre closed her laptop. "It was good meeting you, gentlemen," she said to Nash and Ethan.

"Speak for yourself." Bennett turned and headed out of the room.

"I was." But Dierdre just smiled.

Meena walked them to the stairwell. "The only access to all floors right now is through the front stairwell. This one stops at the third floor." She opened the door and showed them.

Kaleb saw another keypad at the top. "What exactly are you ladies protecting? Is Vanna some rich princess or something?"

"No, because then she wouldn't have lived in a women's shelter for nearly three months," Meena reminded him.

"Right. That." He waited for an answer to his broader question, but she didn't give one.

"Let me know if you get stuck on your next attempt." She gave them a wink.

"Will do." He took her hand for a quick squeeze before following the other two down the stairs and out into the cold night air.

"That was interesting," Ethan said.

"Vanna was in a women's shelter?" Nash asked as they crossed to Kaleb's car.

"They all were a couple of years ago. That's how they all met," Kaleb unlocked his car doors remotely, appreciating having access to his own vehicle, a luxury he hadn't enjoyed in Afghanistan.

"I think you left a few details out of this whole deal," Ethan said. "Starting with that beautiful girl you're obviously gaga over."

Kaleb thought about Meena. He had told himself at first that he just wanted to find her so he could be sure that she and the baby were fine. He wanted to look out for them since Chris couldn't. But now he realized what an idiot he'd been, trying to convince himself that he didn't have feelings for her anymore. Clearly, he was delusional.

He didn't want to get into the nitty gritty, but he gave them a nice general overview—she was the girl who had gotten away, the one woman he had fallen for hard, but she had so quickly belonged to his friend that he couldn't allow himself to think about her like that.

Now his reason for staying away was gone, he needed to decide if the other reasons he had been giving himself were legitimate, or if he should just go for it and see what happened. Would he ruin everything between them if he tried to turn this into more than friendship?

They were nearly to the base when the topic switched back to the dare that Bennett had thrown at Nash.

"All I know is, this is going to be fun." Ethan all but rubbed his hands together in glee. He was all about security and finding ways around it.

"And I can't wait to surprise Bennett with what we can do," Nash added.

That was his two friends in a nutshell. Kaleb couldn't be any more grateful for it.

# Thirteen

SINCE STEALTH WAS LESS important than seeing what was possible, the guys got together around four pm on Saturday—while it was still light out, the cold was bearable, and they were less likely to make a climbing mistake.

Nash had actually managed to borrow the compact launcher, two hooks and ascending ropes and three ascenders with gear from a local man. Kaleb wasn't sure he wanted to ask *why* the man owned three ascenders, but he wasn't going to complain.

"The question is whether or not it's attached strong enough to hold our weight," Ethan said.

"Oh ye of little faith." Nash loaded the launcher with a second hook and shot it up.

Nash gave each line a good, hard tug. "I'll go up first and double-check everything."

They had already put on their climbing gear and he snapped into the two ropes—the first with his ascender and the second like a belay rope on the off chance that something went wrong. A moment later he was ascending up the side almost before the other two could protest—if they had been so inclined. Which Kaleb had not been.

Nash scaled the building quickly—the equipment was in great shape—and he was up and over the wall in less than two minutes. He disappeared for a moment, then popped his head back over the wall, giving them the all-clear sign.

Kaleb and Ethan hooked their mechanical ascenders onto the ropes and were nearly to the second floor when a voice called out, "Stop what you're doing. It's the police."

Kaleb turned and looked at the man on the ground beneath him, gun extended. "Great." He could faintly hear Nash laughing from the roof as he and Ethan slid back down to the officer.

Then there was the clank of metal on metal from the roof.

"Hi, I'm Staff Sgt Kaleb Muller. I'm going to turn so you can see me pull my ID out of my back pocket." He turned and reached two fingers into his pocket to retrieve his wallet and then opened it to show his ID. Ethan followed suit.

"What are you doing climbing the wall?" The man with the tag that read B. Belliston, asked.

"The women who live inside offered to let us use this as a training exercise," Ethan said. Which was more or less the truth.

"Right. If you push the button there on the door for apartment 1, Meena will tell you that we have permission to climb the building." Kaleb really hoped that she would be in her apartment and hear the bell.

The officer did so and waited. Nothing.

"Um, try one of the other buttons. They all know about us." Despite the January cold, Ethan now had a thin bead of sweat on his forehead.

"Right." The officer acted like he didn't believe his story, but he tried a few more buttons.

A second officer, a woman, came around the corner of the building, also with her weapon out.

"I think there's one on the roof, too. The report said they saw a man up there." She looked them up and down, standing in civvies with their hands in the air.

"Yes ma'am, we were just working on our climbing skills. I'm sure if you can reach one of the women - Meena, Dierdre, Vanna, Sheila, Andrea..." Why couldn't he remember the last one's name?

"You could have gotten their names from the news," Officer L. Weight said.

"Yes?" One of the women's voices asked over the speaker.

131

"Hi, this is Lisa, we have three guys climbing the side of your building. They said they have permission."

"I don't know what you're talking about."

Kaleb stepped sideways so he would appear in the camera if she was looking at the feed. "Bennett, I know that's you. Nash is already on the roof, so you're hanging Ethan and I out to dry for nothing."

"Crap. Fine, yes, Lisa, these guys have permission. Dierdre asked them to case the building for weaknesses. I guess you can let them go."

Officer Weight asked, "You were going to let us arrest them?"

"You wouldn't have gotten them into the cars before I came down, I was just giving them a hard time."

"You're sure?"

"Yeah. They've been pretty helpful so far. Wait, how did you get in here?"

"I'm naturally gifted," Nash's voice came over the com.

"I guess he's not on the roof anymore." Ethan laughed.

Kaleb was not surprised. Nash was a devil with a lock pick. He must have been booking it to pick the roof door, rope down to the sixth floor, reach the second floor and pick that lock so he could get to Bennett's apartment.

"We're coming down to let you in." Aggravation radiated from Bennett's voice.

"Good luck, gentlemen." Officers Weight and Belliston headed back to their cars.

"I guess she's not thrilled that Nash was able to sneak up on her," Ethan said.

"Guess not."

The door opened, and Bennett waved them inside. When they came out on the second floor a moment later, Nash waited in the hallway with Sheila and Andrea.

"Where's Meena?" Kaleb asked.

"You probably just missed her, she and Dierdre ran to the store to pick up some items."

"Sure, she says to call if we get caught somewhere, but then she isn't here."

"Give her a break, she's been waiting two days for you to make your move and she needed some things." A smile made Andrea's eyes bounce.

"Bigshot here is gloating." Bennett gestured toward Nash.

"That's because I'm unbelievable, invincible, oh, and *powerful*." He said this with insinuation in his voice.

Bennett walked over and kicked him in the shins again.

He didn't react this time. "I wore shin guards today. Figured that might be your MO."

133

She walked past him and kicked him in the back of the knee, dropping him to the ground. "Yeah, more than one way to skin a cat."

Nash just let out a belly laugh as he pushed himself back up.

"All right, come have a seat in my office," Andrea led them to a different room across the hall from where the women lived and seated the guys at the table she had set up in the middle of the room. There was a computer and printer set up there and a plethora of camera equipment leaned in one corner of the room.

"This is your office?" Kaleb asked.

"For the time being."

"One of the officers said we could have gotten your names from the news. What's he talking about?" Ethan changed the focus of the discussion

"Well, you know, when we were on the news. For winning," Andrea said.

The men just stared at her in confusion.

"The lotto, last summer," she added after a long moment.

"We haven't been here that long and this is the first time I'm hearing about it," Kaleb admitted, rather annoyed no one had mentioned it before.

Andrea folded her hands on the table in front of her. "I suppose Meena has been putting off mentioning that detail. We tend not to bring it up because people suddenly start treating us differently. Last summer the six of us were at an enrichment training—a class put on for women who are or were once living at the women's shelter. The guy was talking about small business loans and grants and waved a lotto ticket at us that one of his apparently idiotic clients thought was a good investment. He gave it to us, and then we won a whole passel of money from it. So we bought this building together and are fixing it up."

It was like little blocks started falling into place in Kaleb's head. "I've asked Meena about your situation here several times and she kept putting me off."

"Life got a little insane after the announcement. We had to wait quite a while for the building to be brought up to code enough so we could move in while they renovate the top three floors for us." She went on to explain their plans for the rest of the building.

"That's a solid business plan," Ethan said. "I'd get the work done on the sales spaces first, if I were doing it as an investment, but it sounds like you need a house more than an investment, so it makes perfect sense to do it this way."

"Gee, thanks for your approval," Andrea said, though she appeared only mildly annoyed at his feedback.

"Sorry, I guess I was thinking out loud. I do that sometimes. My family does some real estate investing, so I tend to think in those terms."

"Then this crazy letter guy isn't the only one you're trying to protect yourself against," Nash said.

"No, unfortunately not."

"Hey, one of the kids said you were here," Meena said as she and Dierdre entered the room.

"Yep. Do you need help carrying anything in?" Kaleb asked.

"There are just a few things left in the garage," Dierdre said.

"We'll go back down with Meena to grab them." Kaleb gestured to Nash, knowing Ethan would be better at prying the info out of Andrea to help them figure out a security plan.

"So, it's your building," Kaleb said to Meena once they were in the elevator, headed back downstairs.

"Um, yeah. How did you find out?"

"Well, the cops who tried to stop us from climbing the building let a few things slip, and Andrea laid it all out for us."

"After my amazing entry on the second floor, via the roof, thank you very much," Nash said.

"Wow, that's impressive. I guess we need to pump up security there."

They stepped into the cold outside air and walked

around to the garage. "Locking it completely off would be best, but I guess you need to access it in case the AC goes out or something."

"Plus, we're going to put up a railing and use it as outdoor space." She used her key card and code to get into the garage. "It can be hard being in public, wondering if someone is going to try to get to the kids for ransom or something, and we have a couple of women who are a little camera shy. Having our own outdoor space where they won't be photographed or hassled is a priority for us."

"Then we'll find a solution that works for you." Nash took the offered bags of food and headed back outside, leaving Kaleb and Meena alone in the garage.

"Why didn't you tell me?" He knew that it hadn't been long and trust took time, but their lotto win was common knowledge so it wasn't like she would be able to keep it hidden for long.

"I was enjoying knowing that you were here because of us, and not at all because of the lottery. I was worried that money would become the elephant in the room once you knew the truth. It's insane how many men started to hit on us once the lottery commission made the announcement."

Since his hands were full, Kaleb simply shook his head instead of pulling her close like he wanted to do. "I don't care if you're barely scraping by or have

137

millions—this is about you and Deven. Nothing could ever make things too awkward for me to not be there for you. After all, we survived dinner the other night."

She grinned and grabbed the last bag from the back of her car.

In fifteen minutes, the perishables were put away, and the adults were back in Andrea's office.

"Andrea said a solid bar on that door isn't going to work," Ethan said when they all settled in again. "So, I'm thinking fingerprints and codes. That way they can't get locked up there if they forget their key card."

"And a panic button to push in case there's another emergency—something that will light up a warning that someone is on the roof." Nash slid into a chair facing backward. "I can just imagine a little kid getting confused and forgetting their code number."

"Good call." Dierdre made more notes on a sheet of paper next to her computer. "I'll check into something like that."

"Speaking of the roof—we'll need to retrieve our gear and lock it up before we go," Nash reminded them.

"Right." Kaleb hadn't thought about that.

"What will you do once Vanna starts having clients come to the side door?" Ethan asked.

"We can set a timer so the keypad will be

unnecessary during office hours, but tenants will still have to have a code to use the elevator or stairs. That way clients will be able to get into the building, but only go to her office."

"Who's going to want a condo in a building that's so secure? This isn't exactly D.C." Nash said.

"Lots of people. Our Realtor has sent out information about the building to other agents in the Kansas City area and has had several bites. It would be at least a year away before they were finished, but there are plenty of people who want the security this building has to offer," Andrea said.

"And that's part of why we're separating our living space so completely from these two floors of the building. No matter who buys or sells this part of the building, we need a secure space," Dierdre explained.

"I get more curious about what you're hiding every time we come here," Nash said.

"We're hiding *us*, from the riffraff. Too bad you already found your way here," Bennett said from the door.

He shot her a grin and waggled his brows. "I think you like riffraff."

"Think again." She crossed to Dierdre and read whatever she had written down and tapped one of the items. "Huh, I hadn't thought of that. Good call."

Dierdre smiled. "Mr. Riffraff made the suggestion."

"Of course he did. Good call anyway. Is there anything else we need to take care of, security-wise?"

Kaleb stepped on Nash's foot when he opened his mouth to respond and Nash closed it again. The look on his face had indicated he was about to pop off with something that would annoy Bennett even more, and they didn't need Bennett belting Nash in the face. Why was it that Nash struggled so much to show he was a mature adult when he was seriously attracted to someone? Not that Nash had said as much, but Kaleb had known him long enough to know what was going on.

"I think we've got it covered."

"Good. Goodbye." Bennett turned and left the room.

"She actually digs me, she just doesn't know it yet." Nash kicked back in his chair.

"And she never will if you don't cut it out," Vanna said. "She's been with egomaniacs before. She's not going to go there again, so start acting like the nice guy you've buried deep inside instead and we'll see what happens."

"Hey, I am what I am." Nash shrugged.

Vanna leaned in. "You're full of crap, is what you are."

Never one to take offense at a woman calling him out, especially when they were right, Nash just grinned.

"Let's book it, dude." Ethan stood and headed for the hall, stopping to say something to Sheila, who smiled and responded before he took off for the stairs on the far end of the hall.

Kaleb followed behind, his hand wrapped around Meena's.

"Come to dinner tomorrow," Meena said to him.

"I'd love to."

"Unfortunately," Nash said. "Ethan and I are working tomorrow night, so you're stuck with only that loser, but you do seem to like him okay."

"So true." Meena gave Kaleb a hug before he and Nash followed Ethan upstairs to collect the gear they had brought and lock up properly.

It had definitely been an interesting and illuminating evening.

# Fourteen

SOMEHOW SUNDAY DINNER preparations seemed more date-like to Meena than any of the other times she and Kaleb had been alone together.

It could be that she actually picked out something datish from her closet instead of letting Bennett badger her into dressing appropriately. It could be that Andrea had offered to host a play date between her son Bobby and Deven. Which meant Meena couldn't convince herself that she had invited him because of her son. Or maybe it was the lily-scented lotion she had slathered all over herself after her shower a little while earlier.

As she set out the candles and lit them for dinner, she remembered their awkward but enlightening conversations the previous week. The fact that he had been trying to flirt with her from the beginning, the way he always complemented her and had talked like she might be his ideal companion. She wasn't about to say the word wife—not even in her head. That thought would lead to her jumping into things before she was ready—something she had done when she agreed to marry Chris after only dating for six weeks. This time, if she and Kaleb had a shot of moving forward, she would take things slower.

"Wow, it looks terrific. You look terrific." Bennett stood at the open doorway as Meena nervously adjusted the flowers in the vase on the counter.

"Thanks, I just, I don't know why I'm so nervous."

"Because he's obviously very into you, and you're worried that he's going to hurt you, not physically, but emotionally. It's scary to trust someone when they've let you down before, or you felt like they let you down before. You need more information before you'll be sure that he won't leave you high and dry again, but I don't think it'll happen this time."

"How do you know he won't hurt me?"

"Because if he does, kicking him in the shins isn't where I'll stop. And I'm not the only one who has your back."

Meena smiled and then the bell for the front door rang. She almost headed down, but stepped to her laptop and clicked the camera icon first, pulling up an image of Kaleb in a blue button-up shirt with the top two buttons undone and khaki dress pants, holding flowers on the stoop.

"Isn't he cute?" Bennett asked, looking over Meena's shoulder. "I'll go get him, but I'm warning, you, if Nash is there to grab me, this time he's going to pay."

Meena chuckled and pushed the talk button. "Bennett's going to let you in. See you in a moment."

"Great," he said.

She turned back to double-check the apartment while Bennett let him in.

Meena heard them on the stairs a moment before they came around the corner into the open doorway. Bennett simply waved, and shut the apartment door, closing them in when Kaleb entered.

Her stomach jumped. "Hi."

"Hi, I love coming up here. Your apartment is so homey, nice dishes, flowers, lit candles. It makes me feel special, like you made extra effort for me. Unless it's like this all the time." He passed over the flowers, a wild mix of this and that with some red roses in the middle. They smelled divine.

"It isn't like this all of the time; I added some touches. I wanted you to feel special and welcomed." Her face heated as she walked around the counter and put the flowers in a simple glass pitcher—the only thing she had that was big enough to accommodate such a large bunch.

"Where's the munchkin?" he asked after a moment.

"At Andrea's. She thought maybe we should spend a little time together without a three-year-old interrupting the conversation constantly."

"That was really nice of her."

"That's what I said." She turned and found him standing about a foot behind her.

"How can I help?"

She gestured to the pot of curried chicken and vegetables. "We'll fill our plates and take them back to the table."

They added a slice of naan bread and a pile of rice to their plates and slathered the curry on top. They spoke of their childhoods, their hopes and fears. She told him stories about the long months of bed rest and time in the hospital during her pregnancy, picking herself back up again with the help of the people in the shelter, who set her on her feet and nudged her in the right direction.

Kaleb talked about trying to get by without Chris in the unit after he died and the struggle those first six months had been. "I was worried about you, and feeling guilty about Chris dying, so it was a rough time."

145

Meena tipped her head. "Guilty about Chris?"

He looked at the fork in his hand, turning it over and over while he spoke. "I was supposed to be riding up front, but the driver and I had been getting on each other's last nerve, so instead of just shutting up and letting it go, I asked Chris to switch seats with me. If I hadn't, he would be the one with you today, eating your delicious curry, instead of me."

Meena thought about his statement. "That's highly unlikely. I would probably just be eating alone right now. Chris and I would not still be married. I realized before he deployed that I had made a mistake. We weren't a good match, which was probably why he started cheating on me almost as soon as you guys shipped out. If we had been together more than four months before the wedding, I might have figured that out before we tied the knot."

Kaleb's head popped up. "He didn't start cheating that soon."

Meena had wondered about that. "He said he did in that last email. Maybe he was just trying to hurt me or something. I don't know, but things were already going south when he left."

"Oh, Chris," he said with considerable disappointment. "That's another reason I have to feel guilty. If I hadn't told him he had to come clean with you, you might not have known, and it wouldn't have hurt you."

"I'm glad I found out, even if he was a jerk about it. I think in some ways it was easier to lose him when I was angry, than if I had just been sad. It was still hard—really hard—but I don't know, I guess I'd rather just know. I'm sure some people would feel the opposite."

"Are you still angry?"

She had asked herself this in the past, and found now that the answer didn't change. "Sometimes. And sometimes I'm sad, and sometimes I grieve over what might have been if he'd lived and we had worked out our issues. And other times I'm just glad that I had him for a little while because that's why I have Deven. I was really angry for the first year or so, especially while I was still dealing with all the Army paperwork he didn't get filed. Accessing his benefits shouldn't have been such a nightmare on top of Deven's health problems as a preemie and having to re-establish my credit." It still frustrated her when she talked about it.

His brow furrowed. "How can you be so calm? You have every right to be furious."

"Lots and *lots* of yoga and meditation."

He huffed. "You want to share some of that with me? Between the PTSD and everything else, I could stand to learn some better coping techniques."

It made her sad to think of the struggles he dealt with. "Do you want to talk about it?"

"Not right now. Someday, though."

"Okay." She was glad she had opted for some nice, comfy slacks instead of a skirt for the evening and that his slacks seemed loose enough for a few moves. Since they had been lingering over their empty plates for a while, she rose. "Let's clear the table and pull out the mats. I'll show you some yoga moves."

"Wait, you want to do it now?"

"Is there a better time to learn some techniques? Do you want to do it after you go home?"

"I guess that wouldn't be very effective." He rose and helped her clear the dishes and food. Then she directed him to sit cross-legged on the floor as she turned off most of the lights, turning on a small one in her meditation corner that diffused a gentle light. Conscious that he watched her every move, she picked up a small decorative bottle that she stashed behind the light, out of sight of the kids and brought it over to sit directly across from Kaleb so their knees almost touched.

"What's that?"

"An attar, which means it's basically an essential oil perfume blend that I use when my head is too full to focus easily for meditation. Frankincense, sandalwood, lavender, and a couple of other things in smaller amounts." She opened the bottle and took one drop, rubbing a little of the diluted mixture along his forehead and dipping a finger slightly below his neckline to rub it along his breastbone. It felt very personal, intimate in a way that they had never been intimate before. Her gaze slid up to his and held while she did the same for herself. His gaze followed her fingers as it dropped to her breastbone, lingering for only a moment before returning his gaze to hers.

She breathed in the earthy perfume, knowing she needed all the help she could get if she was going to focus on anything other than him, sitting so close.

"You always rub this stuff on yourself?"

"Sometimes I use the diffuser and put it into the air, especially if I have to go somewhere quickly and don't want the scent to linger. I find it works best when I wear it. It absorbs through the skin, and through scent. I have a few fragrances I use, but this is my favorite."

"Does it really work?" He looked dubious, but not like he thought it was a useless joke—which was already better than Chris' attitude. "I think it does. If nothing else, using it frequently has helped to train my brain that it's time to unwind and let go of other worries as soon as I smell it. That's useful even if I didn't see other advantages."

"I keep hearing how great meditation is, but I can never clear my mind for long," he admitted. "My thoughts just keep intruding."

"Let's see if I can help you find something that works for you." She lowered her voice to sooth and calm. She considered adding some flute music, but worried that might be a distraction if he was already struggling. "Okay, close your eyes. Take a deep breath in through your nose, hold it, then let it out through your mouth. Imagine that you can see the air as it moves through your body. Clear your mind of everything except for my voice and the movement of the air, in through your nose, down into your lungs, and out through your mouth, cleansing your system of all darkness, worry, fear, guilt. Each breath pushes those feelings away. Be at peace with the universe, pray to your god, or, whatever helps you feel grounded and peaceful."

She joined him in the breathing, though she didn't close her eyes, choosing instead to watch him, to see the expressions flitting across his face. The worry lines softened, the tension slowly eased from his shoulders. She could see him slowly, very slowly, starting to relax as she studied his features in a way that she hadn't allowed herself to do since he had reappeared in her life. His sandy blond hair was growing longer and would need to be cut soon. His lips shifted a little, drawing her attention and she wondered what they would feel like on hers.

*Stop it. Focus on relaxing!*

150

Only a minute passed before he asked, "How often do you do this meditation stuff?"

"Morning and night, just before and after bed helps me sleep better and start my day right." She kept her voice low and soothing.

"You never listen to music or chant or something?" His right eye popped open.

"Sometimes I listen to music. Chanting is like a form of prayer that helps me focus, so sometimes I do that as well, especially when I have a specific need." Deciding music wasn't going to hurt and might help, she unfolded herself and headed to her phone to play some light flute music, turning it down to keep it soft and soothing. "Sometimes, when my brain won't shut down, I find that music will keep part of my brain distracted so that the rest of it can focus on my breathing."

"When do you do yoga?"

"Right after meditation in the morning. You're really not good at being quiet, are you?"

He smiled and tilted his head slightly as he looked up at her. "Not when you're standing there so prettily. And not talking. Your voice is soothing."

"Then we'll do a guided meditation this time. Close your eyes again." She sat in her previous place.

He followed her directions immediately, making her smile. She thought about the issues he said were keeping him up and started there, walking him along the path to self-forgiveness and releasing the guilt over Chris' death. Though she didn't want Chris dead, she was very grateful that Kaleb was alive now. Here. With her. And she wished that when the two men had come into that restaurant nearly five years ago, she had stuck to her first attraction to Kaleb. How different her life would have been with this good man.

When she thought he was fully relaxed, and their work for the evening was done, she slid her fingers over his, since his hands rested on his knees, the palms facing upward. "You did well."

"I just listened to your voice. I think I should fall asleep to your voice every night." His voice was soft and almost dreamy—definitely more relaxed than usual.

"I could record a session for you to listen to." She removed her hands and stood.

"If that's the best I can do." He stood as well, moving closer. "I have something I need to tell you."

"Oh really?" She had no idea what to expect, but his close proximity was definitely making her heart speed up.

"The reasons..." he paused for a moment, and then tried again. "The reason I pulled away from you during your engagement, and even a little before. It wasn't about you. Or at least not the way that you probably thought." He took both of her hands in his, then slid his hands up to her wrists, along her forearms, over her elbows and trailing along the backs of her bare arms to her shoulders. Goosebumps rose on her skin and she loved the feel of his rougher fingers gliding across the sensitive skin of her inner arms. She lifted her eyes to his again, once again seeing a connection there that said he felt the same way she did.

"What was it?" She could barely expel breath as their eyes continued to stay locked together. She thought her lungs might burst if she couldn't make them function, and he was growing even closer. Her lips tingled and she thought she could hear the beat of his heart in her own chest, even though they weren't touching there. Yet.

"I had to pull away out of self-preservation. You see, every time we got together, I fell a little more in love with you. Before I knew it, I was in. All the way, but it was too late."

"You... what?" She was so focused on him and his nearness, she wondered if they had already become one and her brain just hadn't registered it yet. Meditating with him might be dangerous.

"I loved you. I realize now that I never stopped, I just told myself I had, because I needed to believe it. You were everything I wanted and he had you instead, but he was my best friend, so I stayed away."

She didn't know what to think about that, did she love him? She couldn't be sure, it was way too soon. Still... "I wish you hadn't."

Then their lips merged, their bodies melded and she felt his kiss all the way to her gold-painted toes. Every fiber in her being screamed—this guy, he's the one, your other half. The voice went curiously silent while her brain focused on the feel of his hands sliding along her back, the smoothness of cotton under her fingers, his perfect lips teasing hers, the scent of his spicy cologne mixed with the spice of curry in the air. It was everything she had wished and waited for all her life, and yet, completely different from what she had expected.

When a bell rang, she simply tipped her head and kissed him deeper.

They were interrupted by a knock on the apartment door a few minutes later.

"I thought a closed door was supposed to mean go away," Kaleb asked as he trailed kisses down her neck.

She sighed, thoroughly enjoying what his mouth was doing at her pulse point, then pulled back. "They wouldn't interrupt our date without a good reason." Part of her felt like she was floating while the other half of her yanked the first half back to earth. Was something wrong with Deven?

"Sorry to interrupt, only I thought you'd want to see this." Dierdre stood on the other side with a small box labeled "Meena."

She knew who the package was from without even asking. She had seen this brown packaging with the white ribbon before. Nothing else could have brought her back down to earth so quickly and completely. She let out a deep breath. "Come in."

# Fifteen

"I WAS IN MY APARTMENT and saw movement in the video out of the corner of my eye. I glanced over enough to see he had rung the bell and left a package behind before he disappeared. Did he ring your room?" Dierdre asked.

Meena had to think for a moment. She had been so engrossed in the kiss that she had barely registered the doorbell. "I think so. Maybe once, but we were a little distracted." She smoothed the hair back from her face, self-conscious to have been caught making out with Kaleb.

"I can tell." When Meena ran her fingers through her hair, which he had mussed up, Dierdre pointed to her mouth and said to Kaleb, "Your lipstick is a little smeared."

He wiped at his mouth and some of Meena's lipstick came off on his hand. Unfazed, he wiped the other side as well. "Did I get it all?"

"No, you left a little on her mouth, but we'll call it good for now, love." Dierdre stepped into the room and shut the door behind her. "No need to worry anyone else."

"Do you think it's dangerous?" Meena asked, looking at the box.

"You mean like a bomb or block of C4? Doubtful." Kaleb took it and hefted it. "It's pretty heavy for its size."

"I ran it through a scanner Ethan suggested, there are no electronics running in it," Dierdre said.

"I guess we open it, then. Let me." Kaleb stepped back from the women and turned away, blocking them with his body.

"What are you doing?"

"On the very remote possibility that something is rigged in it, no sense in all of us being at risk." He turned back around a moment later, the flaps up on the box to show the contents. There was only a carving inside and a sheet of paper.

Meena reached in and pulled out the white soapstone lotus flower. It was flawless and beautiful, but she didn't want to open the paper. She passed it to Kaleb, who read it aloud.

*Like summer's dew falls*
*On silver grass stems and leaves*
*Your light guilds everything*

157

*On lotus petals*
*Hangs perfection dazzling*
*You're my home and hearth*

*I want to feed you*
*Like summer's dew feeds perfect*
*Lotus flowers now.*

Meena shuddered a little at the imagery. "It's so creepy. How could he think that would make me want to keep this?"

"It looks nice to me, you know, in any other situation. He probably thought you'd like it," Deirdre said. "The carving's pretty."

"I would like the carving, usually. It is pretty, but not from some faceless entity." Meena passed the rock to Kaleb. "Do something with that. I don't want to see it again."

She couldn't stop thinking that whoever he was, this man knew which button to push, which room she was in, despite the fact that she kept her blinds closed at all times. That fact bothered her more than she would tell any of them.

Kaleb waited around that evening until all of the kids were in bed and then joined the women for a meeting. Something more had to be done to protect Meena from this freak.

The stalker hadn't gained entry, so there was that, but Kaleb worried that the man would figure out a way somehow, even if he and his friends couldn't find one that the average human would be able to use.

Dierdre started the meeting by opening her laptop and pulling up the video feed from the front door. "There's not much to see." A figure in jeans and a dark hoodie came onto the steps with a box in his hand. He was tallish and on the thinner side, and kept his face down so the hood covered all of it except a moment when his chin showed. No beard and light skin. He set the box on the stoop and pushed the button to room number one and then turned and sauntered away.

"Did you check for him before you went out to get the box, you know, to make sure no one was going to ambush you?" Bennett asked.

"Yes, I double-checked the area with the feed to my phone."

"Good thinking." Kaleb appreciated her caution, but hated that it might be necessary.

"He really does know which room I'm in," Meena said. "How many people know that? It's not like my blinds ever come up. Not in my apartment, and the window is covered on the ventilation for my jewelry studio, so people can't see in there, either."

"Same here," Sheila said.

"Thirded," Dierdre added.

The others said they occasionally lifted their blinds, but not usually.

"Maybe Deven played in the window sometime. Maybe he overheard something. Maybe it's the silhouette of your hair pulled up in the twist the way you do sometimes," Dierdre said. "There's no way to know, and worrying about it won't change it now."

"On the other hand, maybe he knew the package would get to you no matter which button he pushed, so he just picked one, and yours happens to be the top button. You girls are known to be super close and your name was on the package. We don't even know if he knows it's your room, so let's try not to focus on that. Chances are he's spent more than a few minutes watching this place." Kaleb hated to say that, knowing it would weird them out, but it had to be done.

"The question is how to minimize his chances for contact, and how to figure out who he is so we can shut him down." Kaleb wanted to redirect the worry he saw on most of their faces into something useful by pushing them to form an action plan. So far, they had done well at protecting themselves and each other, but they needed something more.

160

"I'm always a little freaked out about going around the building to get inside from the garage," Meena admitted.

"I thought that was a little odd myself. Is there a way to get through from the garage to the side entrance?" he asked. "I noticed there is a door into the building in the garage."

"The main floor is gutted except for where the side entrance is right now. They put in the stairs and elevator and sheet rocked this entrance before we moved in," Dierdre explained. "They haven't added the door that will go straight to Vanna's office yet, but we could do that so we can trek through the building instead of around. We'll still be living on this floor after she's working in that space, so it's not a perfect solution, but it should solve the problem for the next few weeks anyway."

Kaleb nodded. "Okay, let's start by adding the door now. That limits the possibility for this guy to stop you outside the building, at least until we have to wall off Vanna's office."

"What if—Just a second." Dierdre stood up and left the room, coming back a moment later with the blueprints. She stretched it out on the table and pointed to a spot between Vanna's front office and Sheila's workspace. "What if we added a door here? Vanna can keep sensitive records in the back office, which is hers anyway, and she can keep this door locked during office hours so we don't interrupt her appointments, but the rest of the time we could use it to access the side elevator and stairs."

Vanna tapped the blueprint for a moment then nodded. "I think that will work. Everyone else will just think it's a closet door. Once we all move upstairs, it can stay locked unless there's an emergency or something."

"That sounds like a workable solution." Kaleb debated for a moment before making the next suggestion. "I have one other suggestion that I think will help with security at night."

"I'm already looking at putting up movement-sensitive lights outside," Dierdre said.

He nodded, approving. "Good first move."

"And second?" Meena asked.

He really hoped she wouldn't say no. "I propose that I temporarily take over one of the empty apartments at night. If I'm on site, I'll be here if you need to send someone out in the dark to check on anything that seems off. If it takes a few days to get the garage connected to this stairwell, I can walk you ladies between the garage and outside after dark if needed."

"Do you think we're helpless little weaklings?" Bennett asked.

Kaleb looked at her. "After seeing you handle Nash the other day, I definitely don't think you're helpless or weak."

"He beat me." She looked entirely disgruntled.

"Just barely and you took some seriously good swings. His knee still hurts and that guy could take down a gorilla. If that had been Joe public, you'd have won."

"This is something we have to talk about and vote on," Dierdre said. "It's a really big deal letting someone else into our space, especially a man. The fact that you and your friends were even allowed on this floor is a really big deal."

"I totally get that. I'm happy to step into the hall while you discuss it—or let you have as many days as you need to mull and talk it over. I know you all have bonded and learned to trust each other, and I'm an outside element. I don't want to make you uncomfortable." It was a risk, stepping away voluntarily, but they were a unit, they worked as a unit and he respected that. If he wanted to be part of the unit—which he most definitely did—he knew he would have to let them make that decision; trust wasn't going to come by prying his way in.

"You think we need someone to patrol the halls? Apparently, your stalker can materialize through solid wall." Andrea nudged Meena.

Kaleb glanced back to Dierdre, who seemed to rule when it came to security issues. She nodded him toward the door and he stood and left the apartment, shutting the door behind him. Oh man, he may have gotten used to waiting while in the Army, but this was going to kill him.

He probably should have asked Meena what she thought about his idea first, but he was afraid that she would say no out of consideration for the rest of them. Letting them all discuss it was probably his best bet. If it didn't work, then he would have to think of some other options.

Even though this place was run down and constantly had a layer of dust due to the construction going on, it still felt more like home than anywhere he'd been other than his parents' place. Despite having only spent an hour or two with them, he felt welcome in this circle of women, and after that completely engrossing make-out session with Meena, he finally dared hope that they might work out. He hoped that she would start to love him as much as he already loved her, but he had started so far ahead of her when it came to that, so he knew he needed to be patient and let her figure out how she felt in her own time.

He made several laps of the hall before Meena came out of the apartment where they had been talking. She waited quietly, expressionless, for him to meet her.

"So?" he asked, his nerves spiking.

"We're not really comfortable with the idea of a man being on this floor all of the time. Not when the doors stay open most of the day and we rarely use locks. However, the third floor is also empty. The heat can be turned on in one of the units. The hall will be cold, but it should be reasonably comfortable. If you move into the empty apartment above mine you'll get some warmth rising up from my place. It's definitely not fancy and none of those places have been painted or cleaned, but that's the option."

He wrapped her in his arms. "You have no idea how relieved I am. I thought you all would kick me to the curb. And you came to such a quick decision."

"There really wasn't a downside to it," Bennett said, joining them. "Except if your friends come to visit, but since you'll be on the third floor, that shouldn't be a problem for us. You work on base during the day, so you'll be gone half the time anyway. Of course, if we get too annoyed with you, we'll throw you out on your butt."

"Understood. I'm going to bring Nash and Ethan back to help me block off the door to the roof after work tomorrow. We need to make sure it can't be used to access the building."

"Who besides you mental guys would think of that?" Sheila asked.

"You don't even want to know," Dierdre said as the rest of the women came out to the hall.

That was ominous. "You're probably right that no one would ever try that approach, but I'll feel better when it's blocked. We don't know anything about the stalker. Don't count his strength out until you know for sure that he couldn't find a way."

"Great, thanks for *that* image." Bennett headed for her apartment.

"You're welcome. Besides, once that door is totally blocked, this place is going to be a fortress. It practically is now."

"That was the plan." Dierdre brushed past him and headed for her own apartment.

As the others followed, Kaleb and Meena ambled toward her place. "You don't mind, me staying above you?" he asked.

"Not as long as you don't mind getting up early for morning yoga. It'll be good for your PTSD. We can work on that meditation as well."

He let out an exaggerated groan. "You mean I have to spend time alone with you every morning while you wear tight workout clothes? That's asking a lot."

"I know, it's a cross you'll have to bear."

"Hey, good use of Catholic imagery."

"I've been working on it."

He whirled her around at her doorway and kissed her senseless. Or maybe it was until he was senseless. She was able to do that to him easier than anyone else had.

It was only with the greatest reluctance that he released her, but it was getting late. "Okay, now I better go. I'll do a perimeter sweep before I take off to see if there's anything else out of place."

Meena chuckled. "You're such a military man."

"Hey, paratroopers are tough. That's why you like me."

"It's one of the reasons." She pressed one last kiss to his mouth before sliding away and closing her apartment door.

Feeling lighter and happier than he had in years, Kaleb headed down the stairs and outside, double-checking the door behind him to make sure it shut tight before walking around the building. A sign posted at the entrance to the community garden said the first cleanup was scheduled in a few weeks. He hoped the weather cooperated.

When he got into his car, he stopped to make a few notes about what he needed to bring with him the next night. Then he shot the guys a message to verify they were available to help secure the roof access and move in a few pieces of furniture.

He wasn't leaving anything to chance.

167

SHE SERIOUSLY DID THIS every morning? Kaleb struggled to get through the yoga routine on his first morning in the building. He was in great shape, but by the end of the routine, she was barely sweating and he was a soaked mess, breathing hard. "This is supposed to make me feel grounded?" he asked as they went into yet another downward dog.

"Give it a few sessions."

He glanced over and saw her smirk. "Sure, of course."

"You wouldn't expect to not run for months and then go for a five-mile run without working up to it, and you can't expect yoga to be easy and relaxing the very first time out. Not unless you want me to take it easy on you."

Was she impugning his manhood? "Of course I expected it to be hard, because it's um, exercise, right?"

"It's a discipline, not like anything else you do, I would guess. Shift down and open up." She showed him the next step and he struggled to do it with anything remotely like the grace she always seemed to display.

"Kabe!" Deven's voice said from the doorway.

"Hey there, buddy." Kaleb used this as an excuse to plop on his butt and offer a welcome hug.

The boy ran to him, laughing.

He pulled the boy into his arms. "I'm all sweaty. Sorry about that." Deven didn't seem to mind.

"All right, we'll do a few cool down moves. Get back in gear and ease off, otherwise you'll be stiff tomorrow." She moved back into yet another downward dog.

Deven pulled back. "Doggy!" He leaned over in imitation of his mom's move.

Hallelujah! "That's very impressive kiddo. I'm going to go for a run and lift a few weights first and can cool down after." He stood, grateful for an excuse to be done. No wonder she was so toned.

"That's fine, just make sure you do a proper cool down." She stood as well, pressing a light kiss to his cheek. "I'm making omelets in about forty-five minutes."

"I'll be showered and ready," he promised. "See you soon, buddy." He looked back at the door to see

Meena's arms stretching upward and Deven following suit, doing his best to copy her movements with his awkward, untamed three-year-old body. It was too cute.

He returned to his room upstairs and lifted weights, then ran some sprints in the hall and several flights of stairs before cooling off and stretching, then hitting the shower. He hadn't brought much with him the previous evening besides a mattress and a few clothes—he didn't want to freak Meena out by straight up moving in right away, but he would definitely need to bring a few more things from the tiny apartment he'd been assigned on base.

When he returned to the door outside the second floor and knocked, Dierdre was the one to answer the stairwell door.

"Oh good, I was hoping to catch you before you went to work. How's the apartment? We didn't prep any of the other ones when we moved in since we didn't plan to use them, but we ran a vacuum and wiped things down for you."

"It was fine—trust me when I say that I've lived in much, much worse circumstances."

"Somehow that's not very reassuring." Dierdre handed him a key card. "This is yours, so you can come and go without having to buzz one of us. I set you a pin—it's the first five digits of your military ID number, but we can change that tonight if you pop over. Anytime you use the card to access our floor, the system will send a message to all of our phones so we know you're here. So if you come onto the floor with Meena or anyone else, please make sure to use your card."

"I'll do that. Thanks, this will make things a lot easier. How did you get my military ID number?" He had hoped to be given a card of his own eventually, but hadn't expected it yet. He slotted the card into his wallet.

"I found it when we were doing background checks. This morning I went up to the sixth floor to check the roof access. Looks good. Simple, but effective."

"Sometimes simple is the best route." They had added a bar across the door and added a hook to the door itself, so it couldn't be pulled outward.

"Agreed. We may want to try something similar on this end of the stairwell so we can block this floor off from the rest of the building."

"That's a good plan, since the construction crews use that stairwell. You said you have an elevator going upstairs, right?" He accepted the plate Meena handed him that was filled by a large veggie omelet and toast.

"It goes in next week. The construction manager is anxious for it to be done."

171

"Good. I'll feel better when they stop using the stairwell so much."

"I hear you. Now I've got to see a little girl about school clothes." She headed back down to her place.

"You look so nice in your uniform." Meena adjusted the back of his collar before sitting beside him with her own eggs. Deven was nearly done with his. "What are you up to today?"

"More military brochures. It's exciting work."

She grinned. "Well, as long as your life doesn't get too boring."

"I was ready for a good stretch of boring when I got here." He snuck a peek at her. "Or so I thought. Nothing has been all that boring since I ran into you again."

Looking pleased, she applied herself to her breakfast. Kaleb followed her example. He needed to get in to work. Knowing that he would be back that night made the separation a lot easier.

Wednesday night Kaleb had Ethan follow him home from work. When they came up the stairs, Bennett stood in the hallway at the top, waiting for them, hands on hips. "Where's Tweedledumber?" Today's shirt said "Warning, If Zombies Chase Us, I'm Tripping You."

Ethan paused a second, reading her shirt, then grinned. "Good one. We left him on base this time, but I'll make sure he knows you missed him," Ethan answered before veering toward Meena's apartment. Kaleb followed behind.

"Knock, knock," he said just before entering the open doorway.

Meena looked up from the stove where she was stirring something in a pot. "Oh, hi, Ethan. I didn't realize you were coming."

Ethan slid off his uniform hat. "Sorry, just before Kaleb got off work, I found a possible way to try to track the guy who's been sending you those messages."

"Great. There's plenty of food. Tofu stew," Meena said.

Kaleb glanced over at his friend in time to see a muscle jump in his jaw. "That's so kind of you, but I actually have dinner plans," Ethan said.

Kaleb snorted. He had been hoping for a dinner invite, but if tofu was on the menu, he'd probably just created plans for a burger by himself.

Meena chuckled. "I'm kidding. It's stir-fry vegetables and chicken, it's no problem to throw a little extra into the pot. I was making enough for Kaleb anyway."

"You're sure?" Ethan asked.

"Of course. I always want you to feel welcome here with us. Go ahead and take a seat."

Kaleb came up behind her and slid his arms around her stomach. "You know you don't have to feed me for every meal." Even though he appreciated it.

"Then I won't pack your lunches."

"You know what I mean."

"I like feeding you—especially since you're only here to protect me—it's no more work to cook for three than for the two of us. Next time you could text if you're bringing a friend with you, though." She kept her voice low, so Ethan wouldn't hear.

"Sorry, I'll keep that in mind." He pressed a kiss to her neck, then moved away. He saw Bennett standing in the doorway, watching them speculatively.

Deven ran up to Kaleb, arms extended to be picked up. "Kabe!"

"Hey there, kiddo." Kaleb swung the kid up in his arms and stepped back into the living room while he listened to Deven jabber about his day, even though he didn't understand everything the tot said.

Meena turned to the fridge and pulled out a bag of snow peas, adding a generous portion to the veggies that she had just started cooking in the pan.

"What do you have in mind?" Bennett asked when no one spoke for a moment, bringing the conversation back to the stalker. "Should I bring in the others?"

"Not this time. Meena's going to write back to our friendly neighborhood stalker, and send along a friend." Ethan pulled a flash drive from his pocket. "I have a little program here that will allow us to track him if he opens the picture. If he's using his phone, the phone's GPS should send us a report to let us know where he goes. If he's using a laptop or desktop, it should send us the computer's location. He hasn't actually threatened her, so a restraining order isn't possible, but we could have a chat with him."

"I tried asking him to stop emailing me after the second one, and the third. It only seemed to egg him on," Meena said.

"Then he'll probably be happy to hear from you again," Ethan said. "Maybe it won't pan out, but it's worth a shot."

"Low risk sounds like a good first volley to me." Bennett seemed satisfied and told them all good night before taking off.

Meena finished making dinner and they all sat down to enjoy the meal together. She asked Ethan more about himself, and Kaleb could tell she enjoyed having visitors. She had been such a social butterfly when he had known her before. The stalker, and probably everything else she had been through since he had seen her last, had robbed her of some of that light-heartedness. He was glad to see flickers of proof that it was still there.

175

Once the meal was cleaned up, they settled around her laptop.

"After the last email, Kaleb created a filter so everything from this address goes into a different folder," Meena said as she opened her email. "That way I don't have to see them."

There was a new message in the folder, sent less than an hour earlier.

> Day by day I wait
> For you to see who I am
> Here, on the inside.
>
> Can't you see that we
> Would be perfect together
> My one and only?
>
> Who do you let share
> Your life instead of just me?
> He is not for you.

"Well, I guess we've moved from creepy friendly stalker, to creepy angry stalker." Ethan plugged in his flash drive. "Do you mind if I write the response?"

"Please do." She shifted the computer toward him and picked up Deven, holding him close while Ethan added the worm that was connected to the picture and typed a message.

176

*I wanted to thank you for the lotus blossom carving. It is beautiful work. Did you make it?*

*Meena*

"That's all you're going to say?" she asked.

"It doesn't actually matter what I say, the important thing is that he opens the picture, which is of the carving."

"How did you get a picture?" Meena asked.

"It's at Kaleb's apartment on base. He took it and sent me the image. I wanted stalker boy to feel appreciated a little, that way he's more likely to download the pic and carry it." He sent the email and then shifted the computer back to her. "We're done. It'll notify me when the worm is activated and then we'll see what happens."

"How long will it take?"

"Anywhere from a few hours to a few days. I'd bet that it's less than twelve hours before he picks it up, though. He'll want to see if you responded to his message this time. Have you told the police about all of this?"

"Yes, but not the carving." Meena clasped her hands to her chest, seeming to fold in on herself. "This is freaking me out."

"I sent the information about the letter and carving to the officer over the case this morning. I'm sure he'll want me to bring the carving back with me tomorrow." Kaleb wrapped an arm around her, pulling her closer, wishing he could make her feel safe, but knowing that would only come after this situation was over. She molded herself to his shape, leaning into his chest even though they were still sitting on chairs. Usually she was so strong, standing straight and tall, dealing with her problems head on. Seeing her curled up and vulnerable was painful. He wanted so badly to protect her.

After a minute she took a deep breath, as if steeling herself and then pulled away, banishing any evidence of weakness. "Thanks for doing that. I appreciate everything you guys have done to help us. To help me. It's above and beyond." She stood from the table.

"We hate seeing people suffer if there's something we can do. This is simple, and not nearly as much as I wish I could do," Ethan said.

"Thanks anyway."

"You're welcome, and thanks for dinner. It was delicious."

"You're welcome."

"Can I borrow Kaleb for minute?" he asked.

Meena's brow furrowed for a moment but she nodded. "Of course."

When they came out of the apartment, Ethan

looked down the empty hall toward the apartments where the other women lived, as if searching for someone, but didn't say anything before turning the opposite direction and heading for the main stairwell at the front of the building. "I've been thinking about this door. It has a lock, but the ladies use it sometimes, right?"

"Yeah, to check on how construction is going and the framers will be going up and down it all day, for a week or two until the new elevator's installed. It's a security problem." Kaleb had been mulling options that would work in the short term since they hoped to be in their suites upstairs and gutting this whole floor in eight to ten months.

"Chances are if anyone needs a fire exit, they'll take the other stairwell." Ethan eyeballed the doorway. "But in the off chance that they need this one, we need to make sure that they can get out if they want to. I was thinking about adding a bar top and bottom, but then I realized if it was kids who needed out for some reason, then the upper one needs to be low enough the older girls can get to it, but high enough the little boys can't jog it loose and have it land on their heads."

"We could put the second bar here." Ethan gestured to show where it would cross the door above the doorknob. "And put a latch on it that the little kids can't easily undo. I saw one online the other day. I'll send you a link tonight, so you can get the women to approve it. The lock is working for now, but it might not be enough if the wrong person is determined to get through."

"And who knows if one of the crew might take an unhealthy interest in someone here?" Kaleb had worried that maybe the stalker was actually in the construction crew working upstairs. A background check only worked if the person had been caught doing something wrong. It wouldn't help if this was a first offense, or they hadn't accrued charges for previous ones.

Ethan turned back to Kaleb. "You think more than one guy will focus on them?"

Kaleb shrugged. "I don't know, I get the feeling they were already well on the way to locking this place down as a fortress before Meena told them about the emails. I don't know if there's a direct threat, or if they're responding to what put them in the women's shelter to begin with. Or maybe it's because they're worried the kids could be snatched for a payout after they came into money. All I know is they're scared of something more than a stalker and no one is talking about it. Barring the door sounds like a good low-tech security measure for the time being."

"Sometimes low-tech is harder to get around than high-tech," Ethan agreed.

They turned and headed back for the inhabited portion of the floor. When Sheila came out of one of the rooms, Ethan asked straight out. "Why do I feel like we're trying to block out someone much more devious than just Joe Stalker?"

Sheila didn't look surprised at what would have seemed like an out-of-the-blue question. "We all have a past and secrets of our own."

Ethan nodded. "Fair enough. Do you like pizza?"

"Who doesn't? Round bread, cheese, delicious toppings."

"Wanna join me tomorrow night for some round bread with cheese and delicious toppings?"

With a small exhale that turned her expression wary, Sheila shook her head. "I'll pass, but thanks." She turned and walked into the common room.

"Why do I get the feeling that she's going to take a little work?" Ethan asked as he turned toward the stairwell.

"Probably because she just flicked off your offer of a date as if it was nothing more than a bottle of water." That was interesting.

"Hmm, maybe pizza was the wrong place to start. Maybe I should try sky diving instead?"

Kaleb grinned. "Right, because 'hey, let's jump out of a plane together at twelve-thousand feet,' is far more likely to succeed."

"It couldn't hurt to try." Ethan looked back over his shoulder in the direction where she had just disappeared. "Maybe next time."

"Yeah, good luck with that."

"Thanks. I'm going to head out. See you later."

"I'll watch for that link." Kaleb gave him a wave and heard the door at the top of the stairs click closed on Ethan as Kaleb entered Meena's now-empty apartment. He pulled out the box that had come in the mail that morning from his pack and got to work.

# Seventeen

"CAN YOU BELIEVE ETHAN just asked me out for pizza?" Sheila announced when she rejoined most of the other ladies in the common area.

"That jerk." Meena feigned shock. "How dare he offer to buy you dinner! Why would he think you'd want to spend time with a hunky, adorable, funny, strong, totally smart man?"

Sheila returned to the seat she'd been in until they heard the guys' voices in the hall. "I've so had my fill of men. Yours excluded—Kaleb's handy enough to have around, as long as he remains your problem."

"What do you have against Ethan?" Andrea asked.

"Any guy that self-assured is not for me. All the closet jerks are just sick with confidence." Sheila shifted her toddler, Parker, back into her lap.

"Of course, there's nothing less sexy than a good-looking man with brains and confidence," Andrea agreed.

Sheila picked up the stuffed bunny on the floor beside her and threw it at Andrea. "He's bossy. And annoying."

"And super hot," Vanna chided. "I don't think I've ever heard about you dating. Like not once since we met."

"Just because I choose not to date doesn't mean that I'm antisocial."

"The power word you chose to try and develop more is spontaneous. So maybe you should risk just a tiny bit and try it out," Vanna said.

"Bennett's word is *fearless*, but she still gives Nash a wide berth," Sheila shot back.

"That's because he's a moron. Give me a non-moron and I'll say yes." Bennett tried to look innocent, but the fact was that she never dated either—not as long as Meena had known them. Not for lack of offers.

"Then I have just the guy for you," Vanna said to Bennett.

"No, I'm not one of your clients."

"Neither is he. But you aren't looking for love; you just need a chance to get out and date and he's nice. Not your one and only, but someone to break the ice with. I'm pretty sure the ice is growing super thick considering how long it's been."

"I really don't need the complication right now."

"You and the jerk have been divorced for two years, and your divorce stretched out for like a year before that. You have *got* to date someone eventually," Vanna said.

"Says who? I think I've got a pretty good life without a guy. What if he's Meena's stalker and I give him an in to the building?" Bennett's excuse didn't fool anyone as her fingers started to dance nervously.

"Don't bring him home, then, but seriously, you're not afraid to date, are you?" Andrea threw out the dare.

Bennett had as hard of a time turning down a dare as Nash, but she wasn't biting this time. "I'm not afraid, I'm just not interested."

"Hey," Meena said, remembering why Sheila had stood up in the first place. "What did the guys say about the door?"

Sheila swore softly under her breath. "I forgot to ask—he blindsided me with irrelevant questions. I'm going to get Parker into bed." She stood and adjusted him onto her hip.

Meena saw Vanna and Andrea exchange meaningful looks and wondered why being asked out for pizza would upset Sheila so much. Of the six of them, Bennett, Sheila, and Dierdre were the three who appeared to have gotten out of a dangerous and possibly abusive relationship in the past. Dierdre had been known to date now and then, but the other two never did. Though she wanted to know what was going on in their heads and what she could do to help them find peace, she knew it wasn't up to her. The kind of peace she wanted for them may never be possible. While she didn't think that Vanna or Andrea had dealt with abuse in their previous relationships, she wasn't sure exactly what their burning issues were.

"I better get going too." Meena helped Deven put away the blocks and then excused herself for the night. She would pop over to Kaleb's for a good night kiss—or five—after Deven was in bed.

She got Deven through bath time and was about to settle down with him for a bedtime story when Kaleb called down to her. "Story time is the best. Can I join you?" he asked when she answered her phone.

"Of course."

A couple of minutes later he walked into her apartment, only seconds after the alert that there was a man on the floor dinged on her phone. "Could you hear us from your apartment?" Meena asked.

"Not through the floor if that's what you meant." He pointed to a baby monitor she'd never seen before that now sat on the kitchen counter. "Through that. You can turn it off if you need to have a private chat

186

with one of the other ladies, but if you need me for some reason, I wanted you to just be able to call out and I'll be able to hear you upstairs."

She wasn't sure how she felt about that. "You think he's going to break into the building?"

He walked over and took both of her hands in his. "No, but maybe you'll need help for something else, like killing a spider. Or maybe Deven will have a bad night and I can take him up with me so you can sleep. Look, if you hate the idea, then that's okay, I'll take it back to my room and we'll forget it. I don't want you to feel pressured or uncomfortable."

Meena took a moment to consider the pros and cons. There was no camera and it did have an off button. It wasn't in her work space, and her door was almost always open to the hall, so it hardly impinged on her privacy. "It looks like there's a speaker. Can you talk back to me on it?"

"Yes, actually. But I won't unless you specifically address me."

She kind of liked that idea—being close enough to call out to him if she wanted or needed him while still giving her sisters the peace of not having him on the floor with them. "I'd be willing to try it. Too bad it doesn't have enough range to make it to your office."

"Yes, it is, but that's what telephones are for." He

kissed her briefly, though even that light brush of lips made her long for more. "If you decide that it's too intrusive, just hand it back to me anytime and it's done. No hard feelings."

"Okay. Now, do you want to join us for story time?"

"I'd love to." He took the seat beside them on the sofa and slid one arm around her shoulder. Deven snuggled on her lap and held one side of the book while Kaleb read the story to him and turned the pages. Though she wished the stalker would go away, whomever it was had afforded her this nearly perfect moment, so she would try to focus on the good things in her life.

*The hum of the tank vibrated through Kaleb as he and the other guys in his unit moved toward their destination. Leo and Chris joked about pizza for dinner—not a likely scenario, considering where they were. Chris sat in the front next to Jared the jerk as they traversed the winding mountain road.*

*A moment later there was a deafening noise and flash of light that blinded them all. The tank rocked as the side next to Chris imploded. Kaleb's head buzzed from the loud noise and concussion and it took a moment before he was able to process that they needed to get out of there. Leo sat beside him, slumped against the side wall and Jared hurriedly yanked at Chris' harness. Blood ran down Chris' chest and Kaleb unhooked himself and turned away to pull Leo out of his harness as well. His ears were ringing, but somehow he heard Chris crying out to him.*

Kaleb sat up straight in bed, coated in sweat and breathing heavily, as if he had just run a four-minute mile. The time glowed red in the darkness. 3:17. Well, so much for sleep. The first few weeks back from Afghanistan he had actually slept during the night like a normal human being since that was daytime in the Middle East. Now that he'd been here for a while, his system liked to wake him at weird nighttime hours and insist it was time to be up and working. The nightmarish memories didn't help. The sound of Chris' cries still rang in his ears, even though Chris had been dead the moment the anti-tank gun had hit them and Kaleb hadn't been able to hear a thing.

He heaved himself out of bed and moved to the kitchen for a drink of water. The mini-fridge he had bought for the apartment boasted half a quart of milk and a Pepsi. Caffeine, here he came. He cracked open the can and took a long pull on the soda, appreciating the soothing cool liquid.

Though his heartrate slowed after a few minutes and the sweat cooled on his body, he still felt tied up in knots. Deciding a run might do him some good, he changed into workout clothes and headed out to the pavement.

Thankfully there hadn't been a storm in over a week, so the pavement was dry and clear despite the freezing temperatures. The small town was asleep with only the rare car passing him on the street.

He got in four miles before he returned to the building. All of the lights besides his own were off and he swiped and keyed past the door, heading up the stairs, doing ten flights between the first and third floors before calling it good.

It was coming up on four thirty, so he pulled out his weights and added an upper body workout.

A rustling noise came through the baby monitor and Meena's voice whispered. "Are you up, Kaleb?"

He stopped mid-curl and set aside the weights. He moved to the handset and pushed the talk button. "Yeah, I'm sorry, did I disturb you?"

"No, I wasn't sleeping anyway so I got up to make tea and heard some light stepping noises."

"Sorry, I must have been noisier when I set down my weights than I thought."

"You want to come down for some yoga when you're done?"

He was already worn out, but he might as well. "That sounds great. Give me ten minutes." The yoga and meditation never seemed to work for him when he tried it by himself, but she had a soothing presence. Her voice, her scent, and the peace he always felt in her apartment would ease his soul. He hoped. The desperate need he'd felt to work off the memories that had returned as bright and terrible as the day they had happened had mostly left him, but he craved human contact, and most especially hers.

"I'll be ready for you."

He smiled and finished his reps with more energy than before. He wondered if they would let him rent a room and stay after all of this was settled.

# Eighteen

**I'M BRINGING ETHAN for dinner.**

The message had been left on her phone two hours ago, but Meena had just seen it after finishing up a new pair of earrings—a design someone had paid her to make for their fifth anniversary. Setting down her phone, she held the hook ending and gave the fall of crystals a little swing with an index finger. Lovely. It looked just the way she had imagined. She might be a tad behind with dinner, but she was still pleased with what she'd accomplished that day.

It was nearly five, so Kaleb would be getting off work and Deven would be getting hungry soon. She should do something about dinner.

She had been sure to stock plenty of ingredients lately, on the chance that Kaleb would invite one of the guys home with him, and he had brought over groceries a few times as well.

Instead of an Indian dish this time, she opted for a more American meal. Andrea had taught her the keys to perfect mashed potatoes and gravy—which she knew Kaleb loved. With a side of chicken, a salad and some veggies, it would be a perfect meal. With the help of her pressure cooker, she could have it done quickly.

She wanted Ethan in a good mood—either he was coming to say that he'd tracked the stalker, or that he hadn't, and they needed to try something different. She knew Kaleb checked the filter in her inbox daily to see if there were any new messages, but if there had been, he hadn't said, and she hadn't asked.

The guys came in, their uniforms a little worse for the wear after a long day of work. "Hi, go ahead and have a seat," she offered as she whisked the packaged gravy mix in a pan while it heated and thickened.

"Something smells fantastic." Ethan stuck his head into the kitchen area and let out a gusty sigh. "Oh yeah, I'm really going to have to earn this meal."

"Give me some news and we'll call it even."

"Just news, regardless of whether it's good or bad? You're too easy to please. Can we help set the table?"

"That would be nice. This'll be done in a couple of minutes." She hummed to herself as the men set the table and played with Deven while she finished cooking. They were happy sounds, which filled her heart despite the impending discussion.

Ethan waited until everyone had nearly finished their dinners before bringing up the stalker. "The worm I planted fizzled."

"It didn't work?" Disappointed, she set down her fork.

"Either he didn't click on the picture, or he has some software that's blocking my worm from getting information out. I'm guessing it's the first option."

"We knew it might not work out." Still she had hoped this would be over soon.

"Since that was a bomb, I wanted to try something else. Maybe we could lure him out of hiding," Ethan said.

"You don't think that would be risky?" They had already encouraged the guy by emailing him back. Did they really want to poke the dragon?

"We can manage the risk, keep it small. It's not like we would let you be in any danger. We just need to get him face-to-face to deal with him."

She didn't think she liked the way he'd said that. "This isn't an Afghani soldier you can just shoot out of your way."

Kaleb set a hand over hers. "Honey, we know that, but we have to know who he is before we can do anything about it. He ignored your requests to stop, he's sent you presents and two more emails since we sent the picture last week."

The thought made her stomach twist. She had asked Kaleb to deal with the emails and not tell her. "Maybe we should just ignore him. He hasn't hurt anyone." Maybe they were overreacting, maybe nothing would happen if they just let it go. Except she knew that wasn't true, she just didn't want to risk anyone else getting hurt.

"Babe, he's very upset about me being here. In your life. We can't do nothing because he's going to act sooner or later if we don't change things somehow."

She narrowed her eyes at him. "You didn't tell me that."

Kaleb nodded slowly. "I didn't want to worry you more than you already are. It's not like we learned anything except that he hates me. Considering the way he apparently feels about you, that was inevitable."

"That's a pretty significant thing to learn and not share." She should have insisted on checking the email herself, but it had been easier to abdicate the responsibility with everything else taking up space in her head.

Apparently feeling that they were getting off track, Ethan brought them back to the point, pulling a sheet of paper from his pocket "Since we're going to have to draw him out, I thought maybe we should try writing him back in haiku. Maybe that would speak to him more than prose. I've been working on this one all day. It seems like it would be easy, but it turns out to be tougher than I expected."

"I thought you were at work all day," Kaleb said.

"I was watching the monitors in the prison. Trust me when I say that there was plenty of extra brain power available for writing poetry. I'm not claiming that it's *good* poetry, but you can suggest revisions if you want. I'm usually better at limericks than haiku."

It looked like he had done plenty of revising already. There was a lot of scratching out and rewriting across the page.

After taking a look at it, Kaleb nodded and passed it to Meena for approval.

*With ev'ry letter*
*Sent from your talented hand,*
*My heart races more.*

*I open my mail*
*Wondering what is in store,*
*Enchanting suitor.*

*I hope to meet you*
*One day soon so your anger*
*I can soothe. I'm yours.*

Meena read it twice, debating word choice before passing it back. "Other than the last two words, I think it's fine. I do not in any way, shape, or form want to tell him that I agree I belong to him."

"Good point. What do you suggest instead?" Ethan asked.

Kaleb took the paper and crossed out the line, changing it to:

*I'll soothe, hope restore.*

"It's only marginally better but it's an improvement." She wondered if there was a better solution to this problem. She decided there probably wasn't. "Let's go with it. You know I'll never be able to enjoy haiku again."

"There go my plans for our fortieth wedding anniversary." Kaleb shook his head mournfully. "I was going to make all of those attending write their words of congratulations in the form of a haiku."

Meena craned her head around to look at him. Fortieth anniversary? Was he giving her a heads up that he was thinking marriage, or was that an off-the-cuff joke? She was so not ready to talk about marriage. It hadn't even been a month since he had come back into her life, and though they saw each other every day now that he was living in the building—often morning and night—she definitely needed more time before she started thinking about marriage. She shifted to pretend that she hadn't reacted to his words, but she knew Ethan hadn't been fooled, and Kaleb probably noticed as well.

Ethan folded the paper back into his breast pocket and picked up his fork again. "We'll send it after dinner." He forked up some potatoes. "You could do limericks for the anniversary instead, they're a lot funnier anyway."

"Great suggestion." Kaleb added some more potatoes to his plate and when Deven called out for more as well, he served the little boy too.

Meena narrowed her eyes at Kaleb thinking about how very wrong a limerick contest could end up going. "Remind me not to let you plan any party for any reason in the future, unless me or one of my sisters is there to keep you in line."

"Spoil sport."

"Yep, that's me." Meena passed him the country gravy for his and Deven's potatoes.

"So, now that issue is settled, what do you think it'll take to get Sheila to agree to a date?" Ethan asked Meena.

Meena looked Ethan straight in the eye. "Untapped wells of patience. And try to make her laugh as often as possible. No one I know needs it more."

He nodded. "Patience and be funny. How do I know what she thinks is funny?"

Meena wanted to help him, but she also thought he would need to figure it out for himself if there would be any chance of things working out with Sheila. "Look, just be yourself. She really doesn't date—like *ever*. Not once since I met her, and she doesn't respond to dares like Bennett, so that's not going to work. Be her friend, make her laugh, and maybe—if you're really lucky—before your assignment in Leavenworth ends, you'll convince her to go out with you."

Shaking his head, he said, "I can see you're doing your best to encourage me."

"Just eat your dinner. You can create a plan of attack later." Kaleb scooped up another fork-full of mashed potatoes.

Meena smiled, wondering if there was anything she could do to help nudge Sheila toward Ethan, or if that would end up having the opposite effect.

# Nineteen

TWO DAYS LATER WHEN Kaleb checked Meena's email, there was a response from the stalker.

*Someday you and I*
*Will meet when the moon is high*
*Until then patience*

*Our star-crossed love*
*Will come in line in good time*
*For the lovers' day*

"For the lovers' day?"

"What's that?" Meena asked when he spoke that last line aloud. She was preparing dinner on the other side of the kitchen counter.

"The lover's day. He said he would meet you on 'the lover's day.' "

She stiffened and looked at him. "Valentine's Day?"

"That would be my guess. That's only nine days away."

"You knew that without doing any math? Very impressive." Meena gave Deven two of the snow peas she was preparing for dinner. He took them over to the cars he was playing with on the rug and munched while he turned the carpet into a race track.

"The guy on the radio said something about it this morning." Plus, Kaleb had been thinking about the upcoming celebration. What was he going to do? Would she want something really formal and overblown, or would she rather he put together something simple here in one of their apartments? Planning a surprise without keeping the woman in mind was a recipe for disaster.

Now his mind would be focused on the stalker instead of celebrating. What was this guy going to do on Valentine's Day? Would he try to get her to meet him? This email had been much happier, less angry than the previous ones. Had writing him back in haiku helped, or had it just been the sentiments that the lines had expressed that calmed him down?

"Well, we're going to have our own Valentine's Day celebration here."

It took him a few seconds to process what she had

just said and return to the celebrational plans. "I was wondering about that—your place or mine?" He waggled his brows.

Meena lifted her brows in response. "I meant everyone, with the kids."

"Oh right, the kids." Well, there went that plan. Maybe February 15th instead? It would be easier to get a decent restaurant table.

His disappointment must have been easier to read than he'd have liked because she walked over and took his hand. "Not that I don't want to spend time with you. We were planning this before you became a big part of our lives." She leaned down and kissed him briefly.

Fair enough. "Then maybe we can celebrate the day after Valentine's Day?" he asked when she pulled back.

"That sounds good. We'll avoid the crazy rush."

That was settled. Now he just needed to figure out the perfect late-Valentine's celebration. Oh, and make sure the stalker didn't visit on the fourteenth, or got caught. Either way was fine. That was sort of important too. He pulled out his phone and shot Nash and Ethan a group message.

**Hope you don't have any V-Day plans. We may have an unwelcome visitor over here that night and I could use some extra help with guard duty if you're available.**

Meena returned to the stove, giving the vegetables a stir. "After dinner you should go check out the work the construction crew has been up to. The electrical downstairs is almost finished, and Andrea's apartment on the fourth floor is fully framed in, plus the common area, and Sheila's is started."

"Are all of the upstairs apartments going to be the same layout?"

"No, we all set up our layouts differently to reflect our needs and interests. Sheila and Andrea both have creation space on the first floor, so their apartments will be a little smaller and we'll have shared space for all of us to meet in right in the center of the building, kind of like apartment twenty-three across the hall now, only bigger and more sensibly laid out."

"I'd love to see some actual plans."

She gestured to her laptop. "There's a copy on the computer in the desktop folder labeled blueprints."

He found detailed plans plus notes on the first, fourth, fifth and sixth floors, but nothing for floors two or three. "Are you still discussing what to do with this floor?"

"We have that basic layout showing how the floors will be cut up into condos in another document. As the Realtor sells the sections, the new homeowners will plan the layouts and get approval from the city. Once we've sold enough of them, and moved upstairs, we'll frame everything in and the last couple of apartments will sit empty until someone buys them. Or we may break down and build them out on spec and sell them after the fact, it depends on the bank balance at the time. We just have to make sure there's a background check and rules for the HOA before we put any of the units on the market."

Kaleb's phone buzzed.

Nash: **Spending V-Day with Bennett? You're on.**

Then it buzzed again.

Ethan: **Sheila won't be able to send me away.**

Relief poured through him. Kaleb: **Great, I'm counting on both of you. I'll forward the latest email from jerkoff.**

"What's that?" Meena asked, noticing his distraction.

"Nash and Ethan are both willing to do some guard duty to help watch for your little friend on Valentine's, so you and the girls can fully focus on the kids." He forwarded the email and closed the browser, standing to walk over to her. "I hope that even though our special day will be the fifteenth, that I can at least get a kiss from my Valentine."

She set down the paring knife in her hands and melted against him, wrapping her arms around his neck. "I think I might be able to manage that."

Goosebumps slid down his neck as her fingertips rubbed the short bristles of hair at the nape of his neck. Her lips slid onto his and he all but drowned in her taste, her touch, the faintly exotic scent of jasmine that always seemed to follow her.

He filled his hands with the silky shirt that fell smooth down her back, molding her taut muscles. When he held her like this, he couldn't imagine how Chris could ever have cheated on her, how any other woman could possible match her, even in a small way.

"You guys are always kissing now." Caelan's voice said with the snottiness only a five-year-old could carry off.

"Not nearly as much as I'd like," Kaleb said softly as he pulled away. He let his hand slide back to Meena's hips and turned to look at their unwanted chaperone who stood just inside the open apartment door. "Did you need something?"

"Mom said to come get you guys to see something on TV."

He wondered if she meant the computer monitor—was there something going on outside?

Meena stirred the food in the pan, removed it from the heat, and turned off the stove while Kaleb scooped up Deven and his cars.

In the common room, they found all of the women gathered around the television someone had mounted to a wall. It was a news story about someone who had created a huge banner with a Valentine's haiku on it and draped it over an overpass.

*So you'll know It's real*
*Valentine's means I love you*
*Meena be my girl*

"Meena's your name," Bennett's daughter Grace said. "Is it for you?"

Kaleb forced a smile. "Of course not, there are lots of Meenas out there. I bet he caught her attention."

"In haiku, even," Bennett said, meeting his gaze. "Yes, I noticed."

He'd gone public. There were only nine days until the showdown. Could they figure out who he was before then?

*Dear admirer*

*I saw your message*
*On the highway overpass*
*Your declaration of love.*

*Tell me more about you*
*And how we did meet one day.*
*Fate can be fickle.*

Kaleb hit send on the message the next morning. He had already been working with Officer Lisa Weight—Sheila's sister-in-law—to see if anyone driving along the freeway had seen this guy, or remembered anything that would help them track him down. So far there had been no useful sightings, though.

He had already been upstairs that morning to meet all the construction crew working in the building, even though nothing pointed to it being one of them. Meena had such little contact with people from outside her little world here, content to create beautiful jewelry, raise her son, and support her sisters. He couldn't imagine who else she might have interacted with enough to make them think she was interested in them.

Come to think of it, he didn't think she had been anywhere but the grocery store in weeks. He wished he could take her up on the roof, but even if the weather were nicer, the construction crew hadn't rebuilt the stairs yet. Maybe they should have that prioritized. As the weather warmed in the next month or so, the women and kids were bound to get cabin fever if they couldn't at least get outside.

In the meantime, Kaleb decided Meena and Deven were due for a trip out of this place and started mulling over some ideas. As he stood and checked his watch—it was time to head in to work—he noticed Meena doodling at the dining table.

"What are you working on?"

"I have a client who has commissioned a few pieces. He asked me for a new design for his lady. Something in gold with red and blue stones. He's realistic enough to accept less expensive gems and even made some suggestions. He found a couple of images online and wants me to create something unique along that vein. Also, he wants it for a Valentine's gift."

Kaleb came around and looked over her shoulder at the drawing she'd been working on, noticing the sinuous way the chain twisted and twined around the stones. She was remarkable. "Can you get the stones in time?"

"Yeah, I'll need to go to Leavenworth to talk to a guy I know who sells crystals, jewels, and polished rocks. Lapis Lazuli will be too light colored, but there are some other options."

"I want to see that necklace when it's done." He paused for half a second, considering before throwing out a thought that had been bouncing around in the back of his head for a while. "Also, I'd love to see your idea of the perfect engagement ring."

She stilled for a moment. "That's rather subjective."

He took the seat beside her, waiting until she looked up from what she was doing. "I don't mean a general idea of what's perfect. *Your* idea of what's perfect."

She leaned slightly away, putting more space between them, though Kaleb didn't think that she realized she'd done so. "Kaleb, I'm not there yet, with us. I mean, I love having you here, such a big part of our lives, and you're so great to spend time with, and you love Deven and our chemistry is just off the charts but—"

He silenced her with a light touch of his finger on her lips, knowing he was rushing this and wanting to give her an out, while making sure she knew where this was heading for him. "How about this. When you think you're ready to discuss what this topic implies, you can give me your drawing and then I'll know. Until then, you can think about it, and design, and dream, and I'll let you have time and space to figure it out at your own pace." Even if it killed him.

She still looked a little uncertain, but some of the tension left her shoulders. "Okay, I think I can do that."

Time to change the subject to give her a break. "I heard the construction guys arrive a little while ago. You promised to take me up and show me around one of these times. I have a few minutes if you do."

"Sounds perfect." Meena combed out her hair and put it up in one of those twisty ponytails that boggled his mind, but seemed so effortless for many women. Kaleb scooped up Deven and they headed up the stairs to the 4th floor where the men were working. The men had started furthest from the stairwell first and worked through the common area before starting on Andrea's suite, which would be at the front of the building.

"It's coming along nicely, isn't it?" One of the young workmen said, greeting Meena and Deven. He gave Kaleb a curious look.

"It sure is, Mikey. The plumbers are almost done downstairs!" Obviously Meena was excited for that.

"Definitely coming along," the foreman called out.

"Don't let us get in your way," Meena said.

Having memorized every detail on the blueprints, Meena walked Kaleb through the floor, from a safe distance from the construction in progress, pointing out rooms set aside for bedrooms and kitchens, as well as the common spaces for them all. Next they moved upstairs to the floor above where she laid out her own future apartment, which they would start framing in by the end of the next week.

"That's a lot of space," Kaleb said. "More than Andrea and Sheila."

"They're getting their extra work space on the main floor. Mine will be up here." The gigantic, empty floor was about fifteen-thousand square feet. An insane amount of room by most people's standards—and about twenty times as big as the apartment where she and Deven slept now. She did a little twirl, extending her arms outward as if embracing the possibilities.

After a few minutes they headed back down the stairs to the second floor. "Do you need to make a trip into Leavenworth to talk to the stone guy?" Kaleb asked as he held open the door to her floor.

"Yes."

"Can you arrange to meet with him tomorrow at the end of the day? I'll take you and Deven and then we can go somewhere fun and away from this building. You need to have a break from this place now and then." He locked the door behind them and then set down Deven to put the bars back on the door and latch it down for security while the little boy ran down the hall toward Meena's apartment.

She smiled. "That sounds great."

Kaleb pressed a kiss to her lips. "Perfect. Let me know when you set things up and I'll plan what comes after." Time to do some research.

# Twenty

KALEB HADN'T BEEN OUT the door for more than fifteen minutes before Andrea walked into Meena's apartment. "Family meeting as soon as the girls are in school."

"Um, what? Why? There's nothing new."

"No, but there's something, or rather some*one* sexy and funny and insanely in love with you that we all want to talk about while he's not here. Ergo family meeting. I'll chase you down if you don't meet us voluntarily."

"I'll keep that in mind."

She had less than ten minutes before she heard Dierdre and Bennett returning after walking the kids across the street. Resigning herself to whatever it was they wanted to discuss, she gathered Deven and headed for the common room.

"Court is now in order," Bennett said as soon as Meena walked in.

"Court?" This was new. What had she done? Did they think Kaleb was around too much?

"Yes, we are here to convict one Mahendran Anik Sharma Bertrand of being in love with a nice guy and not trusting herself enough to admit it."

"What?" Okay, that wasn't so bad.

"Oh come on," Bennett said, slouching onto the chair beside Meena. "I heard him essentially ask you to marry him this morning and you basically brushed him off. Granted, you haven't known him long—this time—but you're all but living together now and you knew him well once. I'm the last person to push you to be with someone who isn't good for you, who doesn't love you, or won't take excellent care of you. If you don't love him, then we'll help you kick him to the curb if you want us to. We just want to make sure that you're putting him off for the right reasons."

"There are right and wrong reasons?" Was it crazy that she was amused by this conversation?

"Totally. For example, a right reason would be because you don't love him, or aren't sure how you feel. A wrong reason would be because you're afraid that this man, who has loved you for how many years?"

"Four and a little bit." If her math was right.

"Right, four years—just tell me that you aren't thinking somewhere in the back of your head that he's going to leave, reject, or hurt you like so many idiots have done to us before. Including his idiot best friend."

Meena tipped her head back to stare at the ceiling. Leave it to Bennett to be utterly frank. It was one of the things Meena both loved and hated about her the most. "Thanks, I feel better being reminded about how unlovable I am."

"You are anything but unlovable." Andrea leaned over and put her hand on Meena's knee. "You're the sweetest, kindest, funnest person I know."

"Hey, what am I, chopped liver?" Sheila protested. "Surely at least one of those words describes me."

Andrea gestured to Sheila with her thumb "Oh, and you're far less needy than she is, too."

Meena couldn't help chuckling. She *was* worried that Kaleb wouldn't stick, or that she was moving too fast and that had been the problem with Chris. Even though Kaleb's reasons for distancing himself before he shipped out made perfect sense, and no longer applied, part of her worried that it would happen again. Even though he had, in fact, tried to find her after she went dark after Chris died. Even though he had dedicated practically every spare moment to protecting her since he ran into her.

Her parents and sisters had disowned her after

she chose a white Catholic man. Her best friend from high school had helped her get settled in Kansas City, but after Chris died, she had turned her back on Meena. Chris had cheated on her. Kaleb had distanced himself. It seemed like everyone she had known prior to going to the shelter was no longer in her life. Except now Kaleb was back, but could she really trust him to stay around this time? She didn't know.

"Okay, so yeah, that worry is lurking in the back of my head. What if I get totally wrapped up in him and then he disappears? And even though my heart knows that he would never have tracked me down and stayed with me for our money, considering how much has happened, I have a really hard time believing that he loves me for me, and that there isn't any other reason—like guilt that he lived instead of Chris or I don't know, whatever.

"I'm telling you babe, he's your guy," Vanna reassured. "I know it's hard to trust, we've all been on the losing end of that word, but he's the real deal."

"What, do you read auras or something?" Not that Meena believed in that kind of thing. Exactly. But she didn't *not* believe in it either.

"Nope, but there's a reason my matchmaking record is so high. I know people, and I can read them clearly," Vanna said.

"Just think about it," Andrea said. "Make sure that if you turn him away, it's for the right reasons, and if you're going to do it, do it soon. He's obviously totally into you."

"If you decide to kick him to the curb, that's okay too, that's why we have each other," Bennett said.

"Being with the wrong guy is way, way worse than being single, so don't feel like you have to be with him just because he's being so white knight-ish," Sheila said. "But that doesn't mean that there's no guy for you. Just because I haven't ever found a guy who could be trusted in a relationship doesn't mean they don't exist. Theoretically. And I haven't seen any of the warning signs that I totally ignored with Rod."

Meena crossed her arms over her chest. "Aren't you all supposed to be having this talk with Kaleb, promising to make him pay if he hurts me? I thought that was your job."

"Oh it is, and no worries, if he hurts you, he'll never see us coming." Dierdre's smile was a little scary—or would be if Meena were the target.

"So, are you going to design your own engagement ring?" Bennett asked.

Somehow the whole ring question was so much less shocking and overwhelming than it had been before. Knowing that they all had her back—even the ones who apparently had horrible relationships with men—made her feel a lot better about the whole situation. "I think I am. I have a little free time today before we go pick up some stones for my next project."

"Good. Creating a design will give your brain time to twist around the idea to see how it tastes, listen to the music of your heart, or whatever crap people say when they're trying to be poetic." Bennett stood and stretched.

"And now that we've talked her issues to death," Sheila interjected, "We still have three little ones running around today and we all have work to do."

"I can take them all this morning while I doodle some new jewelry designs," Meena said.

"I can take them after lunch for a few hours. That should give you both a good chunk of time to deal with your torches and hot metal if that's where you are at. I can't wait to see the new railings you're making," Andrea said.

Sheila grinned. "They're going to be spectacular. I'm drawing the full design on my table this afternoon if anyone wants to stop by and see it full-scale. I'll start twisting the steel for the curls before I take a shift with the kids. No hot work today—I'm saving that for later."

"I'll stop over later," Andrea said.

"I'll cover after-school hours until it's time to break for dinner," Sheila said.

Everyone chimed in with their needs and plans

for the day and Meena headed back to her apartment for her drawing tools to take the first shift. With a little luck she would actually get to draw between mediating the three boys' disagreements.

# Twenty-one

WHEN NASH LEARNED that Kaleb planned to take Meena and Deven out for a few hours on Friday night, he insisted on coming by the building to "keep an eye on things for the other ladies."

After getting the go ahead from Meena, who presumably spoke with the others, Kaleb called Nash to give him the okay.

"Perfect, a whole evening around Bennett," Nash had said.

"Unless she makes you stay on the third floor or boots you from the building entirely and makes you stand guard from the street instead."

"She likes me, she just doesn't know it yet." But Nash's voice seemed less certain than usual.

Kaleb shot him a doubtful look. "I'm pretty sure that if she likes you, she knows it. She doesn't seem like someone who isn't sure of her own mind."

Leaving off the bravado he so often wore, Nash sat back in the chair across from Kaleb. "We both know she's mostly ticked at me because I tackled her on the porch. If I can get her past that hurdle, maybe she'll actually give me a chance."

Kaleb wasn't sure where this laser-focus was coming from—Nash had never dated a woman for all that long, or seemed bothered when a woman blew him off. Not that he was a player, he just didn't seem to see a point in pursuing a relationship if they didn't click. "Keep dreaming, but you can chill at my hovel when she objects to your charm." Fancy and overly comfortable were not adjectives he would use to describe his accommodations in the ladies' building, but he had a chair now and his computer so Nash could chill and watch something if he needed to retreat.

"Will do."

They got up to Meena's apartment and she looked up and smiled when they walked in. "I thought you said you were bringing Ethan."

"No, I said Nash." Kaleb had mentioned the name on the text, right?

"Yes, well, if Bennett asks, I'm going to tell her that I thought you were bringing Ethan, no matter what it says on my phone." She winked.

220

"Who's the matchmaker here?" Nash asked, grinning.

"Still Vanna. This is in no way matchmaking. Behave yourself—seriously, I think there's a non-cocky, nice guy buried under there. Bring him out a little. That will earn points with everyone." She patted him on the shoulder as she walked past, grabbing two coats that hung on a couple of hooks by the door. "Deven's in the common area."

After collecting her son, they entered the stairwell to the outside door just in time to hear Bennett say, "Hey, who let you in?"

"We're getting out of this place in the nick," Kaleb said.

"Hear, hear."

They came out into the foyer and exited through the door to Vanna's office to take the back way to her car. "Tell me about this stone guy."

"He's been collecting, polishing, and selling stones since he was a little boy, so for about a hundred years. He doesn't deal in a lot of precious stones, mostly semi-precious to common. If I have to send off to somewhere else for parts for the necklace, I won't have time to get it done and will have to refund the client, so I'm hoping he has what I need. Since this client has purchased several items from me in the past few months, I hate to disappoint him."

"But this store owner, how long have you known him?" Everyone in Meena's life was on his radar right now as possible suspects, even if the guy was ancient.

"Oh, a couple of years. Finding his shop was actually one of the reasons that I delved back into jewelry design. Just wait, you'll like him."

The little shop was just around the corner from where the two of them met a month ago, tucked back on a side road. "How did you find this place?" Kaleb asked when he was unbuckling Deven from his car seat.

"The internet. You can find *anything* on there. Maybe you've heard of it."

"Ha, ha." Worried about busy little hands, Kaleb carried Deven inside. He followed behind Meena, who greeted the old man behind the counter the moment he came into view. "George, it's so great to see you."

"Ahh, my favorite jeweler. Come in, come in. What can I do for you today? You brought a friend with you."

She gestured behind her. "This is Kaleb and the little one there is my son, Deven."

Kaleb smiled, greeting the man. "It's good to meet you, sir, she speaks very highly of you and your inventory."

George looked tired, but he smiled brightly

"That's good. I have some very fine new stones in today, but first, are you looking for anything specific?"

Leaving them to discuss rocks, Kaleb scanned the store—it was small, but a display in the middle of the floor nearly hid a younger man, probably in his mid-twenties who stood behind another counter working on something.

"I have a client who asked for a piece with some blue and red stones. Smallish, probably between one and two karats each. Common to semi-precious and with good, strong color if possible."

"You're in luck, I have just the thing." George opened one of the cabinets from the back and shifted around a little, confusion on his face. "Charlie, do you know where the red carnelian went?"

The young man came around and poked through the display, coming out with the tray of stones after only a moment. He spoke in a slow halting manner. "Sorry, I must have shifted them too far away. These are really nice. We also have some nice kyanite that would probably work." His eyes lifted to Meena, focusing on her.

"That would be perfect." She leaned over the counter and picked through the available stones, selecting ones that were close to the same size and quality from each tray.

Kaleb took another long glance around the store,

then returned his gaze to the trio at the counter. When Deven reached for an amethyst geode on the shelf in front of them, Kaleb stepped back and handed him a matchbox truck he had stuck in his pocket when he stopped at the apartment to pick up Meena. He did his best to split his attention between the boy and what was going on at the counter.

"This must be special, this project for your client," Charlie said. "Is he a good one?"

Meena glanced up at the young man. "He has ordered several things now. He's very particular about what he wants, and he's been a very good client, so his wish is my command."

"We haven't seen you for a while, have you been too busy with other projects to need more supplies?" George asked.

"I've been playing with mixed metals a lot the past few weeks, and using the stones I bought last time. I'm really happy with how they turned out."

Kaleb watched while they chatted. Meena was friendly and open with both men, but stayed focused on the reason they were there. Charlie watched her every move and anticipated her needs—a good business practice, though maybe a little over eager. Not that Kaleb could blame him—she was beautiful and vivacious, especially when she talked about things she loved. Deven chattered and pointed at every display they passed as they walked through the store, his truck clutched in his left hand.

Meena finished the transaction and said goodbye. Kaleb led the way, looking up and down the street before they stepped out. He was being hyper-vigilant—probably more than the situation warranted, but he didn't want to take any risks with Meena or Deven.

"Can I drive?" he asked.

She shot him a sideways look. "It's my car."

"Yes, but I'm the one who knows where we're going." He had studied the route on the map earlier and thought he could find it himself, though he was ready to hit the start button on his map software if he ended up needing help.

She kept the keys clutched in her hand. "So, tell me, and then I'll take us there."

"That would ruin the surprise."

She stared at him for a moment before setting the keys in his outstretched palm.

Not letting down his vigilant scans of their surroundings, he got them seated in the car and he breathed a sigh of relief as they pulled onto the road. He left Leavenworth behind, watching for any cars that might be tailing them, and passed on by Crystal Creek, heading south into Kansas City.

"Where are we going?" Curiosity filled her voice.

"Do you understand the meaning of the word surprise?" Kaleb took her hand and when she didn't respond to his question, he asked, "Are you happy with the purchases you made? Price and quality wise."

"Yes, actually, I was mostly afraid they wouldn't have what I needed. It is a small store, but the selection was good. I have plenty of metal supplies, so now I just have to get to work."

"Will you be able to finish in time?" He checked the rearview window for a tail.

"It'll be tight. I haven't done anything quite like this before—at least not on this scale—and I'll need to do a practice run with aluminum first. Honestly, the timing will be tight so I might be hand delivering it to the post office where his box is, so that he can pick it up later that day."

"He lives close enough for you to deliver it and yet you don't have a home address?"

Meena nodded. "He said he doesn't want it delivered to his home or his wife might open it. Who knows, maybe he lives out in the boonies."

"There's that." Or it could be for a girlfriend instead and he didn't want his wife to know about it. He brushed off the lingering questions and double-checked the sign up ahead, turning south onto I-435. A few minutes later he turned East on I-70.

"Seriously, where are we going?"

He loved that he'd managed to keep her guessing. "We're almost there. I wanted somewhere fun that he could enjoy as much as we do. That's a tall order, you know."

"Tell me about it."

A little later he wound his way around to the Crown Center and found a parking spot.

Meena nodded. "Okay, this definitely gives us interesting options. I've actually never been here before."

"Really? In almost four years? Then it's about time." He helped them out of the car and took Meena's hand, leading her inside and then checking the map on his phone for directions to the restaurant.

Fritz's Railroad restaurant had a line, but it wasn't too long and he figured they had time before the next item on his list.

"This is cool," Meena said as they got into line. They took pictures of themselves with railroad crossing sign behind them and sat in the Fritz' Express train replica that ran along the length of the line to get in. They didn't forget to grab paper folding conductor hats on their way to their seats.

Once they were seated, they called in their food order from the phone at the side of the table and then talked, watching the train while they waited. The small train ran on tracks high up around the walls of the room, delivering food to the tables when their orders were ready. When it reached the right table, the box of food would offload onto a platform that then slid down to table-height so customers could get to it. Deven was endlessly fascinated by the way it worked, clapping every time it came around the corner.

Though Kaleb hadn't seen any cars following them on the freeway, he didn't let his guard down, watching for anyone who might be paying too much attention to their table. He was pleased with how relaxed and happy Meena and Deven were. They stuffed themselves with burgers and fries and sent images back to the other women, who apparently all wanted to bring their kids for dinner one night.

When they finished eating, he checked his watch and smiled.

"Do you think he can hold out for a while longer?" he asked as they left the restaurant.

"Sure, what did you have in mind?"

He turned left and led the way to the Coterie Theater in the corner. "I checked and they still had tickets for tonight, so I got us some. They specialize in kids shows and I thought Deven would like it."

Meena saw the sign declaring it was an Elephant and Piggie show. "Well, he'll definitely enjoy that. Sounds good."

The theater was small and intimate, the actors bigger than life and great at interacting with the kids while they used the aisles for their performance. Theater wasn't usually his thing, but Kaleb knew that Meena liked it and was surprised at how much he enjoyed the show.

When it was time to go, he was sorry to have to return to Crystal Creek and the light tension that always lived in Meena's shoulders there. If the emails were right, this could all be over in a week.

He just had to make sure that it ended without Meena and Deven getting hurt.

# Twenty-two

ABOUT TWO THIRTY that morning, Kaleb jerked out of sleep to the sound of his car alarm clanging. He rolled out of bed and slid his feet into the shoes nearby, grabbing the gun and keys off the floor beside the bed.

He took the stairs to the main floor in five long leaps and pushed through the door into the cold night air, booking it for the back parking lot.

When he got there, the lot was empty except for his car, which now had a well-smashed windshield.

Kaleb turned off the alarm with his key fob and checked for any signs that the vandal was still around, but found no one. Swearing, he went back to the building, realizing too late that he hadn't thought to grab his key card in his haste. They had been talking about getting him a remote control button to the garage, but that hadn't been set up yet, so he'd still be parking outside.

Seeing a light on upstairs, he backed off and counted windows, then pushed the button for Dierdre's room.

"Yes?" she asked.

"Sorry, I was rushing to find out what was going on out here and forgot my key card."

She chuckled. "I'll be right there."

He wrapped his arms around himself, grateful he had at least thought about shoes, and was glad when she opened the door.

"Nice shorts." She glanced down at the gray Army shorts he had slept in—the only thing he was wearing besides his shoes.

"Yeah, I wasn't really thinking about clothes when the car alarm went off."

She cleared her throat as if to keep from laughing, but it didn't work very well. "So I see."

Thankfully she turned and headed back up the stairs, taking him up to the third floor. Kaleb followed behind, grateful to have a chance to get dressed before calling the police.

"What happened?"

"Someone smashed in my front car window. I've only had the car for a couple of months. My insurance company is going to *love* me."

"Good luck with that." She eyed him. "You might want to put on some clothes before calling the police."

231

"Thanks for the suggestion. And thanks for letting me back in."

She swiped her key on the reader and used her code to unlock the door. "Hey, it's not every day I get to see some sexy man chest, so thank *you.*" She turned around and headed back down to the second floor.

Kaleb shook his head and grabbed his phone, pulling on a shirt and pants while talking to the dispatcher.

Meena's voice came over the baby monitor. "Kaleb, did you have trouble sleeping?"

"You could say that." He depressed the speaker button and soothed instead, "Nothing to worry about, I'll tell you all about it over breakfast."

"Okay. Take care."

"You too. Go back to sleep." He heard the swishing sound of movement through the monitor and then her bedroom door squeaked closed. He knew the damage to his windshield would disturb her when she heard about it, but it was just one more piece in the puzzle. The stalker hadn't done anything destructive before now.

He wondered about cameras that might have seen what happened in the parking lot. He didn't think there was one now—that would change when the new ones Dierdre had ordered arrived—but the city offices were on the other side of the alley. Maybe he'd get lucky.

He donned his coat and headed out to meet the police officer who should be arriving any moment.

It turned out that dispatch sent two police officers—it must have been a slow night.

Officer Belliston and a second one who was about the same age that Kaleb had never seen before got out of their cars and ambled over to take a good look at the car.

"Seems like you're around here an awful lot lately. You move in or something?" Officer Belliston asked.

"Yeah, actually. Up on the third floor. I woke up to my car alarm going crazy about fifteen minutes ago. I grabbed my gun and my key fob, slipped on shoes and ran out here, but whoever did this was long gone."

Officer T. Jackson looked him up and down. "You always sleep in your clothes?"

"Nope, ran back in to dress. It's a little cold to run around shirtless right now."

"True enough. Any reason to believe that you were a target?" He pulled out a camera and started taking photos of the damage.

"Could be. Meena's been getting some disturbing letters and the last couple weren't very happy that I've been around. On the other hand, it could have been some kid just taking advantage of the fact that my car is isolated back here. Which reminds me, can you check to see if the city has any cameras pointed this direction?"

"Will do." Officer Belliston handed him a sheet of paper. "Go ahead and write down your statement. Has Meena reported the issue with the letters?"

"Yeah, Officer Weight has been taking updates for us." It didn't take long, since there weren't many details to share, so soon he was finished with the officers.

"You posted out of Leavenworth right now?" Officer Jackson asked, looking at Kaleb's Army-issued coat.

"Yeah. Been in town only a couple of months."

"Where were you stationed last?"

"Afghanistan."

Officer Jackson smiled. "Did a stint there myself. Glad to be home."

He should have known. "You're not kidding. I'm working in foreign military studies now, so I'll be around for a while."

"Here's a case number so you can file that claim with your insurance," Officer Jackson said, handing him a card.

"I appreciate it. Have a good night."

"Yeah, try to get a little more sleep. I know that's sometimes easier said than done."

"Right." He would try, but that was probably a losing battle.

"I've been thinking," Meena said on Monday morning, joining the other women after the older kids were out the door. "Maybe you all should take a little trip for Valentine's weekend. You know, anywhere that isn't here." The damage to Kaleb's windshield hadn't been irreparable by any means, but it had been enough to make her start worrying about everyone else who lived in the building. After lying in bed for half the night thinking about it, she decided she might as well bring it up with the others.

"Oh, road trip! Where are we all going, Meena? Because you know I'm not going anywhere without you," Bennett said. Today's shirt fit her attitude. "To Quote Hamlet Act II, scene iii, line 87. 'NO.'"

"If I don't stay, he'll know and just come after me some other time. Maybe if I'm here the guys will be able to figure out who he is and stop this whole nightmare."

"One for all and all for one," Sheila said.

"We're a unit, and a unit never leaves a woman behind. Just ask that man of yours," Andrea said.

"Don't insult us by suggesting it again. We're here for you, and we're stronger when we're together."

Dierdre hooked an arm around Meena's shoulder, an easy thing since she was at least eight inches taller. "Plus, when you add up our security system, those three crazy Army paratroopers, and half the police department watching the place—which you know Lisa will totally be on top of—will we really find somewhere safer far away from here?"

Meena glanced over at Andrea at the mention of the police to see her roll her eyes. She was definitely not a fan.

Vanna looked a little like she didn't want to agree, but after looking around at everyone, she nodded. "We said we were going to stick together. It hasn't let me down yet."

As the newest member of their group, and not as tightly connected to everyone else as they were to each other, Vanna was the one who tended to hold herself back. She came from a more upscale background, even if she had ended up with a run of bad luck and in the shelter with them. Adapting hadn't always been easy for her, but she was trying to meld with the rest of the group.

Tears rose to Meena's eyes, fear, gratitude, and lack of sleep all working together. "Well then. Looks like we've got a party to finish planning." They would never know how much she appreciated their sisterhood. Or how much she would keep worrying about them until this whole situation was over.

It had been a while since Meena had made it to one of the enrichment trainings offered to current and former inhabitants of the women's shelter. The move, the stalker, and her growing relationship with Kaleb had kept her busy, and the last couple of topics had not been ones that she needed extra help with.

But Comfrey's email had said that tonight they would be discussing ways to defuse arguments and dangerous situations. Though they generally saw eye to eye and worked hard to respect each other's boundaries, Meena figured that there may be times when she and her sisters would need to step back and come at the issue from a different angle. Conflict management techniques were always welcome.

The class started, as usual, with a round robin of positivity—they each shared something good that had happened that week, even if it was a small thing. Meena talked about the necklace she was creating, happy that it was starting to come together.

Next Comfrey stood up and started to talk about ways to defuse or avoid situations that could become dangerous or abusive.

"We all know that not every situation can be defused, right? If the other person or people involved are determined to be angry or are out of control, it's

237

possible that the only thing you can do is try to get out of the situation. However, sometimes there are techniques you can use to calm things down if getting out isn't a realistic option."

She went on to discuss several techniques from staying calm and open to feedback, addressing the other person's concerns, using a sense of humor and owning up to your mistakes. "Remember that the person wants to be heard. Empathizing with their situation is usually the fastest and easiest way to calm them down. Feeling understood is the most likely way to calm ruffled feathers. Now, I want you to try it out—pair up and practice. One of you take the place of, let's say an angry customer at your job or similar encounter. I'll walk around and listen. If you get stuck in a scenario, we'll talk through it."

Meena turned to Bennett. "Well, we don't have regular day jobs. Do you still remember what it's like to deal with angry customers?"

"Let me think... Yep, pretty sure I still remember stuff that happened only a few months ago."

Meena grinned and they worked on a few scenarios they had dealt with.

"You're supposed to empathize with me," Meena said when Bennett shot her a murderous look after she started a new scenario.

"You're supposed to be doing work scenarios, not

Nash blustering his way around our building. By the way, I still haven't forgiven you for letting him in the building Friday, you fink." She crossed her arms over her chest and glared some more

"I didn't let him in the building. Kaleb did. I *swear* the message said Ethan." She allowed a cheeky grin so Bennett would know she was lying through her teeth.

"Mmm-hmm. You're an underhanded shark." Meena smirked.

"Okay," Comfrey brought the group back to attention. "I see some of us have gotten off track." She shot Meena and Bennett a reproving look, which Meena had to work hard not to laugh at.

Yes, it was only a couple of days until her stalker said they would be meeting, but she didn't plan to go out that night anyway. Having Kaleb nearby so much had been good for her—he made her happy, and despite Bennett's attitude, she had been the one to tell Meena to let go of her fears and give it a chance. If that wasn't a glowing recommendation, she didn't know what was.

Somehow this all had to work out, right?

Usually Meena took Deven with her to enrichment training, but this time Kaleb had offered

to keep her son at the apartments and play with him there instead. Since Deven had been a bit cranky that day and Meena worried he might be coming down with a cold, she was just as happy to leave him at home where he wouldn't get anyone else sick, or be exposed to additional germs.

When she walked up to the open door of her apartment, she found Deven and Kaleb sitting on the sofa reading *Green Eggs and Ham* for what was likely to have been the fifth or sixth time that night if Deven'd had his way.

She leaned a hip against the doorjamb and watched while they continued on without noticing her. Kaleb was so patient, so kind and loving. He used different voices for the characters and expressed appropriate shock and amazement at having a mouse in a house.

Neither of them looked her way, thoroughly engrossed, but Bennett stopped behind her to watch them, then gestured for Meena to follow her. They went to her apartment and she sent Grace in to get ready for bed.

"That was quite a sight," Bennett said.

"It was."

Bennett paced to the end of the room, then turned back to face Meena. "Maybe I should have pulled you aside privately the other day to talk about your relationship with him. I'm sorry if it put you on the spot."

Meena's smile broadened. "I appreciate how supportive you are of me, whichever direction my choices lead me." She and Bennett had been through so much together. She seemed so brash sometimes, but other times, she could be the best friend a girl could have.

"Kaleb has gone out of his way to get to know all of us. Vanna has shanghaied him for a question or two several times. I've watched him, the way he acts when he thinks he's alone. The way he interacts with the construction crew, people on the street, his friends, the kids. Dierdre and Lisa have gone on a deep dive in his background and found nothing to worry about. That doesn't mean he can't still turn out to be a jerk. All I can say is that he's nothing like James. I'm not saying run off to Vegas tomorrow, because I'd be very offended if I didn't get to be there for such an important day."

Meena chuckled at that.

"Be careful, but go with your heart. You have good judgement."

Touched, Meena leaned in and wrapped Bennett in a tight hug. It had been over three years and plenty of therapy for Bennett to get to this point—her husband James had terrorized her for over two years before she had run to the woman's shelter for protection. "You know my judgment led me to Chris the first time."

"Was that really your judgment, because I could have sworn it was hormones."

"They get us in trouble every time, don't they?" Meena said with a chuckle.

Nodding ruefully, Bennett agreed. "That's why I'm ignoring hormones and sticking with my head from now on. It doesn't matter if the guy is hot, smart, built like a mac truck, funny, and totally flirting with me. No hormones allowed."

"You wouldn't happen to be thinking of anyone I know when you say that, would you?" Meena thought it was an excellent description of Nash, in fact.

"No, definitely not. This is a theoretical, non-existent man."

Grace came out in her nightgown. "Mom, are you going to read with me?"

"Of course. On my way," Bennett said.

"I need to go tuck my little monster into bed. Thanks."

Meena headed back to her own apartment where Deven now lay asleep in Kaleb's arms.

Kaleb looked up when she came in. "You were here a few minutes ago, weren't you?"

"I didn't think you saw me."

"He was so close to asleep, I didn't want him to get all riled up again." He stood up easily, slightly shifting her baby in his arms, and carefully took Deven into his room and laid him in bed.

Meena tucked the blanket up around him, kissed him on the forehead, and then followed Kaleb back to the living room, leaving Deven's door only slightly ajar.

She slid into Kaleb's waiting arms and pulled him tight. She had never thought she could have this kind of life, especially not with Kaleb. Here, in the circle of his arms, she felt loved and cherished, and she knew Bennett was right—this man was nothing like the men that some of her sisters had fled. He was something special.

# Twenty-three

KALEB TOOK A PASS around the outside of the apartment building as he had started to do lately at least once per night—often twice. This time as he came back around the front of the building from the far side, there was a police officer standing out front.

"Hi, Officer Belliston, isn't it?"

Though he appeared alert, he didn't appear concerned when he saw Kaleb. "Yes. You seem to spend a lot of time walking around out here. I don't see any ropes to practice your climbing skills tonight. They're still letting you inside?"

"Yep, haven't kicked me out yet. I take a couple of passes around the perimeter each night, make sure the building is secure—"

"And have a real good time with Meena, I hear."

Annoyance crept up Kaleb's back. Was the guy jealous or just protective? He seemed calm and unruffled, but who knew? "I won't apologize for loving her. And nothing is going to happen to her if I have any choice."

Officer Belliston nodded. "Good. I got to know them a little last summer through the community garden and my wife who spearheaded the greenhouse." He gestured to the one parked on the front of the community garden lot. "They're pretty incredible women, but something about this guy's emails gets my back up. Officer Weight has been reminding us to keep an eye on this place. I try to keep an eye out, but I'm glad you're here. They need an extra pair of eyes to watch out. If you ever tell them I said that..."

Kaleb chuckled and held out his hands. "Hey, don't worry about me saying anything, they'd likely kill the messenger."

Officer Belliston nodded.

Kaleb let out a breath. "Something's supposed to go down tomorrow for Valentine's Day. He's been making vague hints; he's cagey and we still have no clue who he is, but he's planning something. My two Army buddies will be hanging around tomorrow night to make sure things stay quiet out here." They started walking again, crossing in front of the building.

"I'll keep that in mind and not hassle either of them."

"We'd appreciate any help you can give us."

They came around the corner and heard a rustling in the bushes thirty feet away. Both men turned toward the sound.

Officer Belliston gestured for silence, then pointed toward the noise that was starting again.

Kaleb nodded, creeping toward the noise. They kept each other in sight as they separated to circle around it. When Kaleb saw someone shift in the bushes, he gestured to Officer Belliston. Using hand signals, they agreed that they would each come up on a side—the brush was too thick for the man to run forward and back wasn't a great choice, either.

For a moment Kaleb thought that the officer was reaching for his gun, but the hand that came up held a flashlight, so Kaleb followed suit, pulling one from his own pocket. He had a gun as well, but no need to advertise that if he didn't absolutely need it.

The man was looking through binoculars at the second floor where Meena's silhouette lay across her window and a few windows down, Bennett had hers open six or eight inches, letting in the cold evening air.

He would never understand women.

With a little nod of his head, the Officer called out "Freeze, Police" and he and Kaleb hit the man with a circle of light at the same moment.

The man screamed and fell back on the ground. "Don't shoot. Don't shoot! I'm not armed." His hands slashed up into the air, fingers splayed, showing his hands were empty.

Officer Belliston sighed. "Mikey, what are you doing here at this time of night?"

Mikey sat up, though he didn't put his hands down. "I was just walking through the neighborhood. It's a free country."

Kaleb stood back and kept his flashlight on the guy while the officer closed in. As he approached Kaleb could see that his other hand had been on his gun after all.

"You were just passing through for the past several minutes with your binoculars looking in women's windows?" Officer Belliston asked.

"Hey, I ain't broken no laws." Now that the officer was close in front and Kaleb approached from the rear, he put his hands on the ground to push up.

"Stalking is against the law, as is peeping in windows." Kaleb should have kept his mouth shut, but he couldn't help it. This punk worked for the construction crew. He interacted with Meena several times each week—maybe every day.

"Hey, I'm just keeping an eye on them. Some dude is living there, probably trying to swindle them out of all their money." He hadn't turned from

Officer Belliston and probably thought that Kaleb was one of the other officers on duty.

Now that the kid was in cuffs, Kaleb came over and flashed his light at the kid's feet where the ground had been stood on so often that it was muddy. "Nice try, bud. Looks like you've been standing here, peeking in windows a lot lately. Is this a favorite hangout?"

Mikey got a closer look at Kaleb and sneered when he recognized him. "She's pretty and she's nice to me. You're just temporary. Everyone knows she'll see right through you in no time."

"Sure, she will. Trust me when I say she already sees more of me than anyone else ever has."

Officer Belliston led Mikey right past Kaleb. "Looks like your work here is done. Go give them the good news. And dude, you have it bad."

"Yep," but he said this softly so only he heard it. Adrenaline was still rushing through him when he hit the top of the stairs. He hurried to Meena's place and scooped her up as she turned to him from the kitchen sink holding a glass in one hand and a drying cloth in another.

"Whoa, what's going on?" she asked.

"We got him. The guy who's been watching you. He was outside and Officer Belliston and I snuck up on him and he's going to jail. You're free."

248

"What?"

She didn't get any more words out because he kissed her, putting all of his extra energy into the move, shifting her back one step and then another until she was up against the kitchen counter. The cloth and plastic glass clattered to the floor as she wrapped her arms around his neck and kissed him back.

"Well, that's one way to celebrate," Sheila said from the open doorway.

Kaleb dropped his head to Meena's shoulder. "Seriously, we need to get some locks around this place."

"I heard that," Sheila said.

"I meant you to." Straightening back up, Kaleb stepped back, turning to face the interruption.

"Did I hear that right? Ben arrested the guy? Who was it?" Sheila asked.

One face after another appeared in the doorway until all the women had pushed into the room, waiting impatiently for an answer.

"It was Mikey from the framing crew, and seriously, Bennett, your window is wide open for anyone to look in here."

"I was just airing out the bathroom from the steamy shower. It's only a few inches and it's not like I was standing in front of it."

"Nash could shoot a grappling hook in your window and be in your apartment in less than a minute."

She let out a disgusted huff. "Point taken. It'll never—*ever*—happen again." She left, presumably to shut and lock the window.

"Wait, Mikey?" Dierdre asked. "Mikey from the construction crew? He couldn't put together a basic Haiku to save his life."

"And yet he basically admitted to having kept this place under surveillance and watching Meena."

Meena crossed her arms over her chest, suddenly looking smaller and vulnerable. "I *liked* him. He seems like such a nice guy. I talked to him almost every time I checked on the construction—which is pretty much every day."

"Just goes to show you can't trust anyone," Dierdre said, then looked Kaleb up and down. "You pass. So far."

"Um, thanks?"

The other women left the room, talking amongst themselves, and Kaleb turned back to Meena, hoping for a few more kisses, but she was pensive now, picking up the plastic cup and drying cloth she had dropped.

Sensing her distress, Kaleb tried to reassure her. "Hey, you should be relieved and happy."

"I am."

He tipped his head to the side, studying her. "Funny, you don't look happy."

She set aside the cup and fidgeted with the cloth, staring at it instead of looking at him. "I liked him, Kaleb. He was a nice guy. I think it's okay for me to question, just for a moment, whether or not I have any clue about people and those I can trust if someone I liked and trusted—again—turned out to be completely untrustworthy. It doesn't matter that I didn't put an enormous amount of trust in him. I believed he was just a nice kid with a little crush."

That was not what he wanted to hear, even though he understood where she was coming from. Did that mean that she was going to take a step back from him because her faith in people was failing?

"Meena?"

She looked up and set her hand on his arm. "I'm relieved, I am. And tomorrow I'll be happy, but for just right now, I can't be completely happy."

He pulled her into a hug for a long moment before asking. "Can I do anything?"

"No. Just make sure we're all locked up like usual and I'll see you in the morning."

"Okay." He hesitated for a second, then pressed a kiss to her forehead. "See you in the morning."

# Twenty-four

MEENA FINISHED PUTTING away the dishes, got Deven into bed, and locked her apartment for the night. Usually she would pop over and say good night to anyone in the common area, but tonight she didn't feel like it. Instead, she sat cross-legged on the floor in her living room and looked at the picture frame that hung over the sofa containing the power word Comfrey had painted for her.

Unshakable.

That's what she wanted to be, but right now, in this moment, her faith in others was shaken.

Yes, she was relieved that the stalker nightmare was settled, but she was still...shaken. Could she trust herself? Could she believe that Kaleb was everything he seemed to be when practically no one else in her life was?

Oh sure, she had her sisters, but would they also

someday abandon her the way her parents, her husband, and her other friends, all had? They hadn't planned to abandon her over the stalker, but when she had been sure that Mikey was utterly harmless, how could she be sure about anyone?

She let out a long breath, and then switched into her comfortable pajamas, and returned to her meditation spot on the floor. If ever she needed peace and perspective, it was now. As she brought her hands together prayer-style in front of her, she repeated an old chant for serenity and self-control that she had heard her mother use for as long as she could remember.

Chris had always found her Hindu religion to be a curious quirk of her personality, maybe even a benign compulsion, as if she were simply double-checking the door three times or had to turn off every light in rooms that weren't being used. It was more than that, though—more than his Catholicism was to him, a man who claimed to love and worship a god he took no time to get to know on a regular basis. How could he possibly understand how much her religious practice helped her?

Kaleb was different, though. As far as she could tell, he didn't see her beliefs as a strange quirk, but as an essential part of her personality. A belief that not only figured into the whole, but shaped her into something different than what she would be alone. He meditated and spent time doing yoga with her. Was that just for her benefit? Did he find some of the peace there that she had been trying to share with him, or was he simply pretending to please her?

She knew he had nightmares. He called out in his sleep. He woke early, sometimes only a few hours after going to bed and moved around his apartment. She never told him that he woke her—she had been a very light sleeper since Deven was born. Hearing him move around actually soothed her back into sleep some nights. The clink of his weights, the soft chant of his voice that she imagined meant he was doing push-ups or something. And once in a great while, he played the soft music she preferred while meditating or doing yoga.

Whatever his actions, she knew they were designed to chase away the dark. He seemed lighter to her now than when she had first seen him again. The lines around his eyes weren't as deep, and she was lighter inside as well.

Perhaps that was why humans were created as opposites—to fill the holes and brighten each other with their opposing charges.

She finished her meditations and short evening stretches, and then stood, sure that he was where he could hear her speak. "Good night, Kaleb. Sleep well." As she always did.

Just before she closed her bedroom door, she heard his return. "Good night, Meena, Sleep well."

And she smiled.

All week Meena felt like she had a time bomb ticking in her head. Six days until he does something. Five days. Four. Three. Two. One. Except that the bomb stopped ticking the night before when the police had arrested Mikey. After meditation and a good night's sleep, she felt refreshed, body and soul, and ready to grab her life by the reins.

Valentine's Day had arrived, and she was grateful not to be alone in the apartment building.

Meena hadn't agreed with everyone else's decision to stay despite the possible risk to them and the children; they weren't as easy to force away as everyone else in her life had been.

Bless them for it.

She spent the morning adding the finishing touches on the gold necklace. It was dainty with swirls and spearing golden leaves, turning the stones into flowers. It was her finest work yet—it ought to be, she had spent twice as long on this one piece as she had originally planned, but making the test version from aluminum took time, so she wouldn't make expensive mistakes with the gold. And here were the results.

255

"You called for some photos," Andrea said as she entered the jewelry studio.

Meena adjusted the necklace minutely on the black velvet display, then turned it so Andrea could see it.

Her jaw dropped. "Oh my word. That is so gorgeous! I can't believe I get to photograph it." She took it over to the corner they had set up together the previous month for taking photos of Meena's work. She could have sworn that Andrea took twice as many shots as she usually did, but Meena could hardly complain. These images could help her get more high-end jobs.

"Was his money good?" Andrea asked.

"I double-checked with the bank today. He paid the second half when I sent him the pictures yesterday. These are going to be so much better than what I took before it was finished—and he raved over them."

"As he should."

"Do you mind watching Deven so I can run errands and drop this at the post office?"

"No problem. He, Bobby, and Parker are playing together just happy as can be. Go ahead and take care of what you need to do."

"Do you need me to pick anything up while I'm out? You said you ordered cupcakes or something."

"Oh yeah, I'm supposed to stop at Sweet Confections to get them. If you could pick them up, that would be great. I just don't have time to make them today."

Meena understood that feeling. "Hey, at least your wedding this weekend isn't a Valentine's Day event."

Andrea smiled. "It was supposed to be, but the bride couldn't get the reception center she wanted for tonight, so no complaints here. I still need to finish touching up her bridal portraits—scheduled practically at the last moment—and print them for the wedding."

"Good luck with all of that. Let me know if you need me to take Bobby for a while tomorrow so you can focus."

"Will do."

Meena carefully packed the necklace in cotton and tissue paper, then put it into a box with her business logo on it. This was why she loved this work—creating something truly special and unique for customers who loved her work, who loved each other.

Then again, maybe she had become a little more into the whole love thing since Kaleb came back into her life. Vanna had been right about him, about them and how good their chemistry was, about how easy it had become for them to talk about everything—family, histories, even the painful pieces of their combined past. He made life better and she had been slowly working on the ring sketch for him. He'd seen it, she knew he had, but he wouldn't ask, wouldn't press, until she gave it to him, to signal that she was ready for commitment. And now it was finished, right here in her sketchbook. She looked it over one more time, satisfied. The engagement ring had curving, swirling lines on each side forming a heart and providing places for a trio of tiny stones on each side with a round one on top. She could imagine a matching wedding band boasting a single small stone to echo the engagement ring, as well as a more masculine version for Kaleb.

She locked her studio door behind her and all but danced up the stairs to his room. He was at work, but she wanted to leave him a little present. Pulling the drawing out of her sketch pad, she set it on the kitchen counter where he would see it when he walked in later that afternoon. It would take a little while for someone to make the ring—unless he let her be the one to make it, but it wouldn't feel so much like a gift if she made it. She knew a few good jewelers in the area—she'd give him their names.

She hummed as she packed her purse, making sure Andrea had updated the shopping app and that she had noted everything she needed to pick up while she was out. It felt good to go out alone, free to be herself, to be out in public, no longer worried about looking over her shoulder constantly. Granted, the issues with being in the public eye hadn't entirely disappeared, especially in her home town, but being out from under the stalker's surveillance was enough for now.

She slid into a basic gray trench coat and added a pair of large sunglasses, and then slung her purse into the crook of her elbow. Just a fabulously happy woman out running errands. She closed the apartment door behind her, hurrying down the stairs and into the garage. The drywall crew were coming on Monday, but the "closet" door to Vanna's office had been added to the plans. Vanna's office would open in about a month and the rest of the floor would be open for business by the middle of June. Could life be better?

First things first, the post office in Leavenworth.

She would just pay for the package at the front desk and ask them to put it straight in his box. Then she'd send him a message to say that it was there. He could give it to his wife and everyone would be happy.

As she got out of her car in the post office parking lot, she was surprised when Charlie from the stone shop called her name. She waved back and headed past the row of empty spots where the mail carriers parked their vans overnight and toward the rock shop's van, which was between her parking spot and the post office entrance.

"Hello, is that the necklace you needed stones for? Is it beautiful?" He pointed to the package in her hand.

She hugged it close, bubbling at the fact that she had finished something so beautiful, that she was out in the open air in public again, and anxious for Kaleb to find her ring design. "Yes, it turned out so perfectly. I'll get the pictures up on my site in the next day or two so you'll be able to see them."

"I'd love to see it, the piece you worked on so hard. Can I see it now?"

She just laughed. "Don't be silly, it's all packaged. I know there's nothing like the real thing, but you'll have to wait for pictures. Your grandpa has the best inventory. I really have to go."

She turned to leave, but he grabbed her wrist with one hand. "Sorry, so sorry. I need you to come with me. I need to show you."

She tried to pull away, confused at his insistence. "Charlie, I can't." But then he was pressing a cloth to her mouth, and pulling her behind the van. He was stronger than he looked. And she was starting to get dizzy. The van door opened and her head started pounding. Pounding. Pounding. The dizziness grew worse and she heard him talking to her as he pushed her and then her legs into the back of the van and the door slid shut.

"Charlie, what's going on?" And why did her head hurt so much? He didn't answer her, but instead flipped her onto her stomach, then straddled her from behind while he pulled her hands behind her. The clicking sound of handcuffs seemed to echo in the empty van and the metal bit into her skin. She took in a deep breath to scream—why hadn't she screamed yet, she thought, fighting through the thick fog taking over her brain. Before she could let out her breath, a rag was shoved into her mouth and something dropped over her head turning everything black.

There was the sound of movement around her, and then the van started to move as she tried to think through her headache and the growing nausea. They drove only a few minutes—she thought it was a few minutes—as she struggled to keep her stomach under control and not retch. Her fear of the whole situation was strengthened by the fear of puking into the rag and then choking on her own vomit.

Her brain had started to clear again when the van came to a stop, causing her head to bang against the metal connector at the bottom of one of the front seats. The front door slammed closed and a moment later the sliding door opened. Charlie's hand wrapped around her wrist and he pulled her to a seated position, all the while apologizing, "So sorry Meena. I had to save you from him. You will be safe here." He seemed to repeat this thought over and over as he helped her stand on unsteady legs.

Meena's stomach still felt sick and her head ached even more after banging into the seat, though her head was less fuzzy than it had been before, whatever he'd dosed her with must have been wearing off. With her head covered, she couldn't see where they were going. The cement under her might have been smooth and even, but her equilibrium was off kilter making it hard to tell as she stumbled. Despite her growing fear, she was glad for his supporting hand under her elbow, which was the only thing keeping her from tripping. She wanted to refuse, to pull away, but between the headache and nausea, and desperate need to keep from puking when her mouth was gagged, it was all she could manage to follow along.

She could hear something squeaking, like a gate opening and the cement ended. Then they stepped onto something softer and lumpy she thought was probably grass. Ten unsteady steps, Twelve. Then he brought her to a stop and she heard the creaking of hinges again, this time they sounded different though and the sound ended with the clatter of wood on rock.

"You must be careful, the steps are very steep. I

will keep you safe." Charlie's halting voice said, then pulled on her wrists again.

Meena leaned back, trying to pull out of his grasp. She shook her head only once before the pounding made that impossible, and she made negating noises in her throat. He was much stronger than he looked, or maybe she was just weaker than usual, because he forced her to follow him down the wooden stairs. She dragged a toe on one of the steps and nearly tumbled down whatever was left, but he held her up, keeping her from landing on her face.

"Sorry, so sorry. I will keep you safe I said. I promise I will too." Charlie's voice sounded more nervous than before, but Meena wasn't sure if that was because this had been harder than he'd expected or because her brain fog was clearing enough for her to sense his nerves.

He released one of her hands from its cuff and she tore at the hood over her face and the gag on her mouth even as he wrestled her other arm to a bed frame, connecting her to it with the second half of the cuffs.

She pulled the gag out of her mouth just in time to puke all over the dirty rock floor. She retched twice, then fumbled for the metal frame of the bed that her wrist was attached to steady herself while she cradled her pounding head with the other hand. The headache had grown with her puking until she almost couldn't think of anything besides that and the nasty taste of bile in her mouth.

In the background she could hear Charlie's voice go up a notch as the situation stressed him out. He started to stutter even more, stumbling over his words.

"You should not do that. Being sick is not the plan. I will care for you."

Charlie pushed her against the bed and she gratefully lowered herself onto the thin mattress. Though the headache still drove like a spike into her brain, it seemed to soften slightly as she rested her head on the pillow, which was surprisingly soft. Her stomach was calmer, with any luck she might not be sick again. She felt shaky and cold—it was still winter, even if February was often less frigid than January.

Meena looked around herself in the fading afternoon light and saw that they were in a combination storm and root cellar. A slice of sky was still visible from the open cellar door and she thought that she should call out for help, but her mouth was still dry and her throat scratchy from puking.

Charlie was scrambling around the floor, muttering to himself as he cleaned up the vomit.

"It will be fine now. I'll care for you always now. We will build a home."

"I just need to rest," she told him, though she was

feeling quite a bit better with an empty stomach. However, if she was going to get out of this situation, she had to take stock, figure this all out.

Taking a closer look at her surroundings, her eyes landed on three very familiar jewelry boxes—white ones with her logo printed on them. Charlie had to be her client. C.H. Andrews.

# Twenty-five

AFTER THE SUBDUED WAY Meena had acted at bedtime the previous night, Kaleb had been worried about how she would feel in the morning, but she had been in a much better mood, giving him hope that everything would be okay. As he sat at his desk trying to proofread a brochure on Afghani troops, he'd realized they didn't need him to stay in the building anymore, not after Mikey's arrest. The women would be well within their rights to boot him back to his place on base, which he had barely stepped into all week.

Still, Meena had kissed him goodbye and said there would be more of that when he got home, so he was hopeful that he might be able to make the move permanent. When he came up the stairs a little after five that evening, he had expected to find Meena at home, but her apartment was dark and empty. He ran

266

upstairs to his apartment to drop off his gear and stopped for a moment when he saw the sketch paper sitting on his counter top. He knew that paper. He'd seen her working on it several times over the past week.

Not sure if he believed what he was seeing, Kaleb set down his pack and jacket, and took the few steps to cross the room.

His hands shook as he picked it up, looking at it more closely than he had allowed himself to do before. It *was* her drawing of the ring! He wanted to go find her immediately and kiss her like crazy but he took a moment first to savor knowing that she loved him and wanted to marry him. He knew she was worried about how fast everything had been going. She and Chris has rushed the wedding because he was coming up on a deployment, but that wasn't a problem now. He could wait a little longer for the wedding, let her really feel comfortable about them, about his complete commitment to her.

Joy rushing through him, he headed back to the second floor and the common room—where she was bound to be.

The place was busy with holiday decorating. Andrea stood on a chair hanging streamers from one corner of the ceiling while the older kids stuck pink and red paper hearts on the walls. Deven saw him and ran over, his arms outstretched. "Kabe!"

Kaleb scooped him up. "Hey, there, kiddo. It looks great in here. Where's your mom?" he asked as if the tyke could explain it to him.

Andrea got off her chair and started hauling it to the opposite corner. "She left a couple of hours ago to run some errands. I thought she'd be back by now, but you know how grocery shopping lines can be at this time of day."

Kaleb pulled his phone out and called Meena, but her phone only rang on the other end before going to voice mail. "Weird."

"Let's see where she's at on her list." Andrea pulled out her phone and clicked on the shopping app the women all shared, and her brow wrinkled. "She hasn't crossed *anything* off her list. Not even the stop at the post office, and she was going to do that first. Maybe the list isn't updating?"

Warning bells went off in the back of his head. "That seems unlike her. Do you know which post office?"

Andrea also looked concerned. "No, but I'm sure you could look it up on her laptop. If you can get into her account, I can find the customer info since we use the same merchandising program. Chelsea, will you keep an eye on the boys, and you all holler if you need anything. I'll hear you."

Kaleb set Deven down to play with the boys again

and returned to Meena's apartment and tapped on the touch mouse, which brought up her screen. He found her—unsecured—password list and signed into her merchant account. Andrea clicked the mouse a couple of times and found the order for the necklace, along with the customer address. The guy who ordered it lived in Leavenworth? He pulled up the last email the guy had sent—C.H. Andrews—and forwarded the email to himself and Ethan. Maybe it was nothing, but it didn't *feel* like nothing. If she was going there first and she hadn't made it... he didn't want to even think about it.

Unable to sit and wait, he made a quick decision. "I'm going to track her trail. Maybe she's having connectivity issues or her phone died or something and she hasn't been able to cross things off of the list." He left the apartment and closed the door behind him, pulling out his phone to try to call again. Still nothing.

"Let me know if you find her, and I'll let you know if I hear from her too," Andrea said, the worry lines around her eyes getting deeper. She opened the app again and messaged him a screen shot.

He waited until it came through, and then pocketed his phone. "I will."

Kaleb had only been on the road for a couple of minutes when Andrea called him. "I called Sweet

269

Confections on a hunch, to ask about my cupcakes. Meena hasn't picked them up yet. I'm really worried."

So was he, and the worry grew worse every minute. "Call Officer Weight. See if they've had anything pop on their system since Meena left. I'll keep in touch." He paused for a second, but added before ending the call, "Also, have someone ask Mikey if he knows what a haiku is."

"Oh, okay."

Ten long minutes later, he pulled up behind Meena's car in the otherwise abandoned parking lot behind the post office. A row of delivery vans lined the side closest to the building, but there were no other vehicles in the lot. He parked next to her car and when he glanced in her window, her cell phone sat on the front seat. The worry that had been building in his stomach shifted into real fear.

Meena's headache had downgraded to manageable and her stomach was calm when she opened her eyes again, but she still didn't have a solution to this situation. Regardless, she had to start somewhere.

"I wondered when you would open those eyes again. My special woman," Charlie said from where he hovered, standing next to her.

She rubbed at her eyes with her free hand, deciding that acting more confused than she already was might help her assess the situation without upsetting him. "Charlie, what's going on?"

"I brought you here to be my one and only girl. You are my whole world. I saw you with him in our store and knew it then, that he would turn you. But I could not let such a terrible fate come to one I loved so. You are safe with me here where no one will see us. Look what I brought you." He gestured to the small table next to the tiny old bed where the last three commissioned pieces she had made were lined up, including the necklace.

She wrapped her coat tighter around her. The cellar doors had been closed and the room was lit only by an electric lantern he had set on a shelf. There was a small gap around the cellar doors at the top of the stairs, which let her know that it would be dark soon. She wasn't sure how long she had lain on the bed, pretending to sleep while she recovered from the drug he'd given her. It had also given him time to calm down, which she appreciated. It would be much easier to deal with him when he wasn't so worked up. "Why didn't you tell me you were my client?"

"I wanted them to be what you would like the best, so you made your gifts."

Something about the way he spoke kept niggling

at her mind, but she couldn't figure out why through the last bit of haze that clung to her brain.

"I said I would be with you on the lovers' day, and here we both are."

The words and the syllabic beats of five-seven-five caught in her head and she repeated his phrase again in her head and finally understood. The stalker had been Charlie all long.

# Twenty-six

KALEB CALLED ANDREA back while he still stood beside Meena's car. Whatever happened, whoever had her, they had grabbed her while she was at the post office. They were in Leavenworth now, so Officer Weight didn't have jurisdiction here, but maybe she could hurry the flow of information on her end. She had to know people at the local department.

"Hey, have you talked to Lisa?" he asked without preamble when Andrea picked up the phone.

"Seriously, she doubts he's even heard of a haiku. They didn't have enough to hold him this long, so he was released early this morning. Dierdre just ran upstairs to talk to Mikey's boss, and hold on, here she comes."

The phone switched hands and Dierdre's voice came onto the line. "The crew is still up there, putting in a few extra hours since they're running behind.

Mikey's been there all day. When I asked him what a haiku was, he was as thick as poundies. Er, he had no idea."

Kaleb let several excellent curse words fly. "Look, Meena's car is still parked at the post office, with her phone on the seat inside. Whatever happened, it happened here. We need to figure out who this C.H. Andrews guy is right away. He's got to be the real stalker. I'm calling the police and then I'm calling Ethan and Nash for backup."

"We'll see what we can figure out here. We're right behind you if you need anything. Bring her home safe."

Kaleb called up dispatch and asked for an officer to be sent to the post office because someone had been abducted from the back parking lot. He didn't answer the dispatcher's continuing questions, hoping the dispatcher would send help immediately if they didn't realize he hadn't actually seen anything. He understood the importance of working within the system as much as possible, but he wasn't taking any chances with Meena. Instead, he hung up the phone and called Ethan.

The news wasn't good when Ethan picked up the phone, diving in with an answer without saying hello. "All I can tell is that the IP address is in the area, and who the internet Service Provider is."

"Well he's got to have her, because she disappeared while mailing the package and no one else would have known that she would come here to deliver it. I called the police, so they'll be here soon."

"Good, if you can convince them that it's urgent, they can call the ISP and tell them they need the address for an emergent situation. If they understand that someone is in danger *right now*, then they'll help us out. Sometimes they require faxed paperwork from the police department, but you might get lucky." Ethan gave him the name of the ISP he needed to contact and then gave him the contact phone number to call.

"Great, thanks. Grab Nash and be ready for my call when we find out where she is."

"On it."

"Here's the cop." Kaleb hung up the phone.

A short Hispanic officer got out of his squad car and approached Kaleb. "Are you the one who reported an abduction?" Officer H. Hernandez asked.

Kaleb wanted to shout, "He's got her, call and find out where!" However, he knew that he would need to make his case before he would get the man to help him. He hoped that the fact that he was still wearing his military uniform counted in his favor and not against. "Yes. Let me give you a little history, you can verify with Officers Weight or Belliston from

Crystal Creek. My fiancée, Meena Bertrand, has been dealing with a stalker for some time. She didn't know who he was, but his emails were getting more pointed and angry. We thought we caught him last night, but now we think we were wrong. She came here to mail a package this afternoon, and was never heard from again. This is her car."

Hernandez looked at it. "Are you sure she didn't just decide to walk off to take a break?"

Anger and frustration boiled inside him, but Kaleb pushed it down and did his best to be respectful. "She has a three-year-old son, she just barely agreed to marry me, like today." Okay, so it was a slight exaggeration, but that's what had been implied by the drawing.

He continued, "She had people counting on her to bring back items for a party tonight. Trust me, she was happy and looking forward to life ahead. She lives in Crystal Creek, but the client said he needed the gift for tonight, so she brought it over here to have them put it in his PO box, because he didn't give her a street address. The only person who knew she would be here this afternoon, other than her family, was the guy who ordered the necklace. And my buddy on base just gave me the information we need for the ISP, so they'll tell us where the guy emailed from."

Officer Hernandez seemed to be following the

line of thought just fine and his eyes narrowed. "So, you didn't *see* her get abducted?"

"No, but I'm telling you, the way to find her is through that IP address. We have filed reports about the stalker, and he broke my windshield last weekend. This is an emergent situation and we really need your help."

"Let me see that." He pointed to the scrap of paper Kaleb had written the notes on from Ethan. The officer pulled out his phone and called the number. It seemed to take forever for him to work his way up the ranks to someone who was able to give him the address. He hung up and looked at the paper again. "Looks like it's coming from over on Shawnee."

Kaleb swore again. "You're kidding me. It's that rock shop, isn't it?"

Officer Hernandez put his hands on his hips. "How'd you know that?"

Feeling like an idiot for not guessing sooner, Kaleb said, "She shops there for her business. The grandson acted oddly. Let's go."

He turned to leave, but the officer stopped him with a hand on his arm. "Hey, I didn't say you were invited."

"Look, I'm going over there to talk to the owner whether you come with me or not, but I'd rather have you there. Meena's life could be in danger. My buddies will be meeting us there. They're MPs on base, but we all know they have no jurisdiction here. We need you so we can keep this all within the bounds of the law." It was killing him to hold back and not just hop in the car and go talk to the old man, but he knew he could screw everything up if anything was done wrong.

Officer Hernandez narrowed his eyes at Kaleb. "I'll talk to the old guy, but you don't have enough proof to search the place without his permission or getting a warrant from a judge."

"I'll get permission." Kaleb thought George had seemed reasonable enough, and no way was he the one who abducted Meena—he was too old and frail for that. His grandson, on the other hand... He ended that line of thought before it drove him mad. "Look, I've stayed calm and respectful with you when that's the last thing I want to do. I can do this and stay in control."

Hernandez eyed him for several seconds before nodding. "Fine, follow me over. Stay calm and let me do the talking or you're out."

Unlikely, but he would give the cop a chance. Kaleb called Ethan and Nash as he hopped into his car and followed the officer over. The guys had been waiting only a few blocks away, so they pulled in before Kaleb reached the sidewalk. "You two wait out here—it's a tiny store and I don't want to overwhelm or intimidate the old man." Not if he didn't have to, anyway.

"Will do," Ethan said as he and Nash got out of the car, and then began loitering.

"Are you their superior officer?" Officer Hernandez asked as he opened the door.

"Not anymore, just their friend, but this op happens to be my baby, so they'll help where I ask them to." He stepped into the shop and wondered if it was more dusty and darker than before, or if that was just his imagination.

Officer Hernandez just grunted and then greeted the old guy. "Hi, George, how are things going today?"

"Just fine. What can I do for you fellows?" He looked more closely at Kaleb. "Don't I know you?" He sat on a stool behind the counter looking even more tired than he had the week before.

"Yes, sir, I was in here with Meena Bertrand the other day. I was holding her little boy."

"Right, her new fella. How is she?"

"Well, that's why we're here," Hernandez said. "Is Charlie around?"

"Oh, no, that young man has found himself a girl. He's been gone all day preparing a Valentine's Day surprise." George looked so pleased by the news that he stood and approached the counter. "It's good seeing him so happy."

"I'm sure it is. Look, does he have his own apartment or a cabin? Somewhere he might go to be alone?" Hernandez asked.

George's brow furrowed, as if confused by the line of questioning. "He lives with me since the accident last summer and we don't have any vacation spots, if that's what you mean. Why? Has he done something? He's a good kid."

"George," Kaleb decided to try a different angle. "Does your grandson like haiku poetry?"

"Why, yes, I didn't think you'd realize that—most people don't. He received a brain injury in the accident with his mom, and ever since, he believes it's bad luck if he doesn't speak in it. Like someone will die." He seemed to want to smile, but couldn't quite manage it. "He's gotten very good at it though it sounds strange sometimes, but not so much that people realize. It's his OCD, ever since the accident."

Officer Hernandez turned to Kaleb. "What does that have anything to do with it?"

Kaleb ignored the question and focused on the old man, keeping his voice low and as casual as he could manage. "For a couple of months now, maybe a little longer, Meena has been getting unsigned emails from someone writing her in haiku. Love notes. Lately they've gotten more possessive and even a little angry, especially after I was in here with her the other day."

George's face fell. "Oh, dear." He felt behind him for the stool that he had been sitting on earlier and slumped onto it.

Kaleb hated to distress this older man when he was clearly not feeling well. "Is Charlie's last name Andrews?"

"Yes, he's my daughter's son. Why?"

The officer had stepped back and let Kaleb continue the questions, which was very appreciated. He continued carefully, "Several times in the past couple of months, Meena has been commissioned to make some unique jewelry. When we were in here last weekend, we picked up stones for a new piece that was ordered by a C.H. Andrews. The emails he sent her verifying that he liked her design came from this shop. A couple of hours ago, she went to deliver the necklace to the post office and no one has heard from her since. We think maybe she's with Charlie."

George's expression grew more anxious by the moment. "You think my Charlie abducted her?"

No use freaking the old man out yet. "Or maybe she went willingly. We can't know unless we check on her. Could we have your permission to check here and your home to see if they're there? We're really worried about her. It would really ease everyone's minds if we knew where she is and that everything is fine with Charlie."

Officer Hernandez shot him a skeptical look, but George seemed not to notice it.

Seeming to relax, George nodded. "Of course. I would know if they were here, but you can look. Our home is a couple of blocks over. There's a key under the mat to the back door."

"I know which one it is. Thanks, George. We'll try not to disturb anything," Officer Hernandez said.

Kaleb felt like one brick had been removed from the stack on his shoulders. Now if they could just find Meena safe and well.

# Twenty-seven

NEARLY AN HOUR HAD passed and Meena's head had almost cleared. Charlie had taken to repeating himself, especially the theme of needing to keep her safe from someone she could only assume was supposed to be Kaleb.

"Charlie," Meena said, trying to convince him not to worry. "I'm fine, you didn't have to save me from Kaleb. He's very nice. And I need to be with my son."

"You and I will start anew with our own family. What happened is over."

Frustration and fear curled through her. He didn't seem angry, just insistent, but she knew people who were unstable often flipped from one extreme to the other with little provocation.

How could she defuse the situation? Then she remembered the words from the class she took a couple of nights earlier. Staying calm and not showing your emotions could help to soothe and calm some people who were upset.

She remembered her power word posted above her sofa at home. Unshakable. She had been trying to practice that, and though she hadn't succeeded last night, this was a new day and a desperate situation when being unshakable was far more important. She could do it.

She had to.

He grew more agitated with her when she spoke normally. Writing him in haiku seemed to calm him. Maybe what she needed to get through to him was to speak in haiku, though she knew that would be harder in practice than in theory. She counted out the syllables on her fingers before she spoke them. "I appreciate your willingness to help me. But I am just fine. My life has become one that I cherish so much and I love my son. Can you see that I do not need your loving help, though you are thoughtful?"

Charlie sat beside her, calmer now, and she did her best not to show how much she wanted to move away from him. He touched her arm. "Your world has become a prison not of your making. I will set you free."

She looked around her at what had to be a storm shelter and wondered why he didn't see this as much more of a prison than the big apartment building that would have an enormous roof garden come summer. "To break me free of my prison up above us, must I stay here now?"

He paused, as if just realizing that there had been a disconnect in his thinking. Then he shook his head. "There is chaos there, world of danger and despair. Safety is found here."

Her heart fell. If he truly believed that it was too dangerous for her to be with others, then there might not be any way to reason with him. Still, she had to try.

Kaleb gestured for Nash to come inside the shop, to keep an eye on George while they checked the place out. Nash entered and started talking to George, keeping him distracted and asking about some of the items in the displays.

Kaleb, sure now that George wouldn't be able to call his grandson and warn him if he were so inclined, cleared the rest of the building with the officer—it wasn't a very large space, so it only took a few minutes.

"He was right, if they were here, he would have known," Officer Hernandez said as they re-entered the store area. "I didn't see a back entrance, did you?"

"No."

They thanked George, and Kaleb gestured for Nash to stay. He nodded that he would.

They came out the front door. "You said you know where George lives?" Kaleb asked.

"Yeah, follow me." Officer Hernandez started radioing in before he reached his car.

"Come on, Ethan, you can ride with me." They hopped into Kaleb's car in the fading light—the sun would be setting in a few minutes—and followed the officer to the tiny house just two blocks from the store, seeing a van parked in the driveway. He gave Ethan the update along the way.

"Could be how he got her away from the post office," Ethan said when he saw the solid-sided van.

"Makes sense. Man, I hope she's here." He had been focusing on the next step for the past hour, trying not to think about what might be happening while he waited, explained, waited, and explained. Now that they had found the place, he was more anxious than ever, wanting desperately to just find her already, and to know that she was all right. He couldn't think about what might be happening to her right now or he would go out of his mind, and this was the most delicate part of the whole search.

"Me too." They got out and followed the officer around to the back door.

"I called for backup," Officer Hernandez said.

"We're waiting for my partner and *you're* staying out here. You handled George well, but the last thing we need is an angry lover shooting first and asking questions later."

Kaleb wanted to protest, but wasn't this why he had brought the police in to begin with? He saw a storm shelter door a few yards away. He might as well put his time to good use. "Fine. Do you mind if we look around out here?"

The other police car pulled in the drive, thankfully without using his sirens. "Sure. We'll call if we need help." Officer Hernandez said this a little cockily, as if he knew they could handle it.

Kaleb was sure they could, especially since his vote was on the storm shelter.

The other officer arrived, and Hernandez explained the plan. They used the key under the mat to go in quietly and Kaleb motioned for Ethan to follow him. "What do you think?" he asked, pointing to the door in the ground.

"Could be. More private than the basement, and the closest neighbors are off a stretch. Betcha Grandpa's hard of hearing anyway."

Kaleb debated for a moment. If Charlie were inside the house, he might see them through the windows and act out before the officers could get to Meena. If, however, he was in the back yard, Kaleb and Ethan might be able to get to her before Charlie realized there was something going on at the house. Both options had some risk. There were no sounds coming from inside the house, and he didn't see any lights on, so he nodded and Ethan followed him to the storm shelter, checking the trees and bushes along the way to make sure there wouldn't be any surprises.

They arrived to find the cellar door wasn't latched from the outside like he'd expected. Kaleb held up a hand to signal quiet and slowly started to pull on one of the heavy wooden doors. He nearly sighed in relief when the door not only opened, but he heard Meena's voice through the slight opening.

"I'm like the robin, needing the sunlight and sun, true signs of freedom." Her voice was soft and low.

"True darkness within," Charlie's voice pleaded. "Light is nothing if not safe from dangerous ones."

Ethan grabbed the handle of the other door. He spoke, barely a whisper, "He might see the light when we open them."

"Maybe not, it's almost dark. I don't want to freak him out. Slow and calm." Kaleb counted off, they carefully opened the doors in unison, sending a shaft of the fading outdoor light down the stairs and then carefully followed it. "Charlie, it's over now." Kaleb said, realizing that Meena had been talking to him in Haiku as well. Trying to put the meter together in his head along with everything else that needed to be done was hard. "She does not want to stay here, in the dark and cold."

Charlie moved in front of Meena, his face defiant, blocking her as if to protect her from Kaleb. "She is my true love, I cannot let her go up to the world above."

"She wishes to live where the air is clear," Kaleb paused, recounting the syllables in his head, "and pure. Listen to her now. Down here it is cold, the icy winds blow much too hard, and it is winter."

Charlie grew agitated and grabbed Meena close. A gun appeared from...Kaleb had no idea where. "You cannot have her. She is everything I need. My home and safety."

Kaleb now had his own gun in hand, though the last thing he wanted on his conscience was another death. He would do it for Meena. He would do anything to protect her.

It was Meena who spoke next. "These men you see here are my friend and loved one. Please let me go with. You are sad, lonely. But this life is not for me. Someday you will see."

Charlie shook his head, his movements erratic. "There's no place for me up there where all thinks me an oddity."

Meena turned her head to better see him. "This

is not the way. Let me go, to live, I pray. My young son needs me."

Kaleb realized for the first time that she was attached to the bed with the other arm. He heard Ethan head back up the stairs and hoped that he was going to tell the officers where they were.

Some of the tenseness in Charlie's demeanor loosened, though whether it was because there was less threat with only Kaleb there, or because of what Meena had said, it was impossible to know. She pushed a little harder. "We can end this now, and you can make a new life, we all suffer strife."

He shook his head, muttering something Kaleb didn't understand.

Perhaps Meena did, because she asked, "Charlie, why do you speak in haiku?"

He sucked in air. "Haiku helps you live. It is breath for all of us. It keeps you alive." Tears started to pour from his eyes and down his cheeks. "Haiku helps you breathe. We need to stay alive too. Stay alive, alive."

"You are not dying. Haiku won't change that at all. Don't you know you live?" Meena asked.

"I need you, someone to stay with me and help me. I cannot be alone." The tears came faster now, though it didn't make him loosen his grip on her or the gun.

Kaleb kept his own weapon in his hand, but he still hoped they might convince Charlie to put his down. "Your grandfather lives. He loves you too and will stay. You do not need her."

"No, no he does not. He is like the walking dead. Come spring he is gone."

Footsteps behind him, ones too heavy to have come from Ethan, had Kaleb shifting to the side to make room for the officer. "Officer Hernandez," Kaleb asked without looking at the newcomer. "Is George dying?"

"I don't know. You can put that down now soldier. Charlie, you don't want to do this."

"I am alone now. You cannot understand how much it hurts for me!" Charlie said in a sob.

"She has a young son," Kaleb reminded him. "Do you want the same for him as happened to you?"

Charlie shook his head, tears still pouring from his eyes. His grip loosened on Meena and Kaleb jumped forward to grab the barrel of the gun, pointing it toward the rough stones of the floor. Upset, Charlie pulled the trigger and the bullet slammed into a rock between their feet propelling bits of rock into the air to bite at Kaleb's legs and arms.

Officer Hernandez took the young man down to the mattress and Kaleb, finding himself in sole control of Charlie's gun, holstered his own and passed

Charlie's to the second officer. "He cuffed her to the bed. Could you release her, please?"

The officer agreed and after holstering his own firearm, he dug into a pocket, and one handed—since he was still holding the other gun—passed the handcuff key to Kaleb.

Meena had jumped out of the way as Officer Hernandez had barreled onto her captor and stood at the top of the bed, out of the way as they cuffed him. Finally, Kaleb was able to get around to her and release her wrist, pulling her close for a hug. "I was so worried about you," he whispered into her hair, holding her tight.

"Me too. Me too." She buried her face in his chest and Kaleb just held on while the officers took Charlie up the stairs and out into the night.

She shivered and Kaleb took off his jacket, wrapping it over her own. It was a cold night, and she had been out in it for close to three hours. "Let's get you inside."

She nodded, clinging to him.

They came out of the cellar in time to see them putting Charlie in the back of Officer Hernandez's car. They radioed something in while walking back to the house.

"You know I have to separate you three for our statements," Officer Hernandez said.

"She's freezing. Is there any chance you could do hers inside?" Kaleb asked.

"I have your coat. You're the one freezing," Meena said, still burrowed into his side.

Ethan joined them. "Charlie's grandpa has cancer. He was given only six months to live—about three months ago."

Meena looked up at Kaleb. "That's when the letters started arriving."

"I know, Babe." He pressed a kiss to her temples and they all headed to the house. Nash and George were pulling into the driveway in George's car and they took everyone inside to different spaces in the small house while they gave their statements. Kaleb ended up in the living room filling out a written report of what had happened.

When the second officer finished with Nash and Ethan, which didn't take long considering neither of them knew much, he came over to talk to Kaleb, gesturing to the written report he had been working on. "How's that coming?"

"Done. You want to ask me some questions?"

The man read the report, then asked a couple of follow-up questions. "You and your friend have very concise reporting styles, clear and straightforward. Makes it easy. Thanks. You handled yourself. Have to admit if it were me, I'd a been tempted to shoot first and ask questions later."

Kaleb allowed a grim smile. "Don't think it didn't cross my mind. Thing is, I've seen some awful things. I was really hoping this didn't have to be one of them."

"Thanks for helping ensure it wasn't. We'll be in touch if we have any follow-ups. You three are free to go whenever you're ready."

"Sounds good. Whenever you finish with Meena, we'll clear out."

He walked over to join Ethan and Nash in the doorway to the kitchen. Movement drew his eye and he looked over toward the stairwell. George sat on the second step, his arms crossed in front of him, rocking slightly and looking ashen. He was already sick—Kaleb couldn't imagine how awful it would be to receive such a blow on top of everything else he was already dealing with.

It only took a few more minutes for Officer Hernandez to finish with Meena. Kaleb was so ready to take her home, but before she allowed him to lead her out of the house, she paused, glancing at George, then sent Kaleb a beseeching expression.

He wanted to get her out of there, but he knew she was safe, and if this helped her find some kind of closure, he didn't want to deny her the opportunity. Instead, he nodded and allowed her to pull away and walk over to George.

"George, are you okay?"

His gaze lifted to her face. "Of course. But you, he... I'm so sorry, Meena."

Meena set her hand on his shoulder. "I'm okay, George. He did his best to be careful with me. He said you're sick."

George nodded. "I'm only working half days. He was going to take over full time next week, but now I don't know what will happen." He slid his old, withered hand up to cover her hand on his shoulder. "I'm just glad that you're okay. You're a good girl. You take care of yourself. I'm sorry."

"Me too." She stood there for a long moment before backing away, returning to Kaleb. He pulled her close, holding her tight for another long hug. She was safe. He could deal with anything as long as he knew that. "Come on, let's go home."

She bit her lip. "I want to, but I still have errands to run."

He couldn't help but laugh—even after everything she'd been through, she was worried about picking up cupcakes. "Everyone's waiting for us at home."

She checked her pockets. "But I need to pick up stuff for the party. Where're my phone and keys?"

"Your phone is in your car. Let's see if we can find your keys." Kaleb pulled her close to his side.

They found her keys in the back of the van while

he tried to figure out how to get her home as soon as possible. He wanted her home, safe, surrounded by her sisters. "Okay, I'll make you a deal. Nash and Ethan can run the errands that have to be done tonight and meet us back home with whatever you need."

She paused to debate for a moment, which made him wonder if the errands had been an excuse to put off dealing with the aftermath of her feelings, but then she nodded. "Let's get my car—I need the list. Did I leave my phone in there?"

"Yes, you did."

After picking up her car and arranging for the guys to make a Sweet Confections run and bring Kaleb's car, Kaleb and Meena soon pulled into her parking spot in the garage.

"Do you need anything before we join the party?" He knew the adrenaline would be wearing off soon, if it hadn't already, and wanted to give her a minute to deal with her emotions first if she needed it. He had already messaged Andrea to let her know that they were coming home, and Meena was safe, which she had thanked him for, profusely.

Meena tucked her hand under his upper arm. "I just need to hold my little boy and hug everyone in sight. I'm fine, really."

"You're amazing." He could hardly believe

Meena had come through all of this so well. He figured there would be flashbacks and nightmares in her future, but she was dealing, much better than he'd expected. Or maybe she was doing her best not to deal with it for now. "Unshakable, even," he said as they got into the elevator.

She pushed the button for the second floor. "Not even close. I was shaking like crazy on the inside, especially after you came down those stairs. I was so afraid he might shoot you."

"It's not what's inside that counts in this case. You kept it together. You defused the situation. I'm so proud of you." He pulled her close and kissed her softly just as the doors opened.

"Ugh, seriously, what's with all the *kissing*?" Caelan asked.

Meena just laughed. "Kissing is fun, especially when you're kissing the right person."

"Mommy, mommy, mommy," Deven came running. "I missed you."

"I missed you too, sweetie." Meena swept him up in a tight hug, already looking happier.

"Where are the cupcakes?" Caelan asked.

Meena took her hand and turned toward the common room. "Sorry, I got waylaid. Nash and Ethan are bringing them in a few minutes."

Caelan half walked, half danced her way down the hall. "Okay, then. Everyone's waiting for you."

Everyone else was gathered in the common room playing games and eating pink mashed potatoes and heart-shaped chicken nuggets. Meena passed Deven to Kaleb and grabbed the first sister she saw, who happened to be Vanna, in a hug. There were hugs all around as she moved from person to person, though the kids were confused, since the adults hadn't explained what was going on.

Nearly fifteen minutes passed before the speaker from Andrea's apartment across the room buzzed. Andrea hopped up and asked, "Who is it?"

"Did someone up there want cupcakes?" Nash asked.

"Seriously?" Bennett crossed her arms in front of her "I'm Sorry For What I Said When I Was Hangry," tee, turning to glare at Meena. "You really invited him? I mean, Ethan, okay, but Nash?"

Laughing, Andrea went to let them in.

"You may have to get used to him," Meena said, touching Kaleb's arm. "I gave Kaleb my ring design today."

"Really? That's great! Congratulations." Bennett gave them both hugs.

"I haven't asked her yet. It's not official until I do, and it's been kind of a busy evening so far." He didn't intend to let much time pass before he did make it official, though.

"Then how about if I ask you?" Meena asked.

Enjoying the byplay and grateful beyond words, Kaleb decided to play along. "You can't ask me, I'm the guy. I'm very sexist when it comes to this. It's definitely the man's job, and I haven't done it. I'm not even prepared. You only gave me the design today, and I thought it would take a lot longer for you to get around to that."

Meena looked up at him through her lashes and hugged his arm. "Is there really better timing than this? Everyone's here, we're safe, the sword of Damocles is no longer hanging over our heads. Plus it's Valentine's Day. If you don't do it, I will—I'm not at all worried about your sexism."

Man, he loved this woman.

"Hey, why isn't anyone waiting to mob us for cupcakes, did we pick them up for nothing?" Nash called from down the hall.

"Hurry up," Dierdre said to them from the doorway, "Kaleb is about to propose."

Apparently, he was getting engaged. Right now. "Okay, now it is." He waited a moment for his friends to come in the door—might as well let the whole gang watch this. He slid off his chair and onto one knee and looked Meena in the eye, taking her hands in his. "Mahendran Anik Sharma Bertrand—seriously, that's a lot of name. I have loved you almost from the moment I first saw you, nearly five years ago. I cannot imagine ever living apart from you again. You make me feel whole. Will you marry me?"

The smile that split Meena's face brightened the whole room by at least a hundred lumens. "Yes. Yes, I'll marry you!" She slid onto his knee, wrapped her arms around his neck.

Kaleb slid one arm around her waist, pulling her a little closer, and set his lips on hers, first a soft feathering across her lips. Then leaned in and let the sweetness of their kiss slowly unravel, keeping in mind that they had a dozen people watching them. He whispered against her lips. "I will love you forever."

"Ditto."

"Ugh, seriously? More kissing? Are they every going to stop?" Caelan asked someone.

"No, honey, I hope they don't ever want to stop," Bennett's soft voice responded.

Kaleb pulled away—reluctantly—and whispered, "I won't ever want to stop."

"Me neither."

Nash waited three heartbeats before asking, "Okay, seriously, no one wants cupcakes?"

Kaleb and Meena just laughed. This was one rowdy, complicated, eclectic family, but he wouldn't give it up for anything.

Coming this June

# Spontaneous Love

Book Two in the Shelter Sisters Series

Love is not on Sheila's side. She isn't sure if she just has terrible taste in men, or if she actually changes nice guys into total jerks, but she's done with romance. Her resolve hasn't been challenged for the past three years—but that was before she met Ethan Wolf.

Ethan's time as an Army paratrooper is nearly at an end and he's making plans to settle down in the area to start a security company. Intrigued by her from the start, he's glad when she takes him up on the offer to help her install the new railing in the apartment building she owns with friends.

When her abusive ex-boyfriend shows up again, Ethan is determined to protect Sheila and her two kids at all costs.

# Acknowledgments

This new series has been a lot of fun and only possible with the help of many people. First, big thanks to my two brothers-in-law, Konrad Wilson and Jonathan Buttrey who helped me out with some research details. Thanks to Danyelle Ferguson for editing along with my amazing grammar team, Cathy Jeppsen, Julia Lance, Kayla Sharp, Lori Banister, Diana Shanks, Brooke Heaton and Gretchen Stopyra.

Big thanks to Pauline Buttrey for keeping so many of my publicity balls in the air so I could focus more on writing and as always, the biggest thanks to my husband for always being my biggest supporter. Love ya!

## About Heather Tullis

HEATHER TULLIS has been reading romance for as long as she can remember and has been publishing in the genre since 2009. She has published more than thirty books. When she's not dreaming up new stories to write, or helping out with her community garden, she enjoys playing with her dogs and cat, cake decorating, trying new jewelry designs, inventing new ways to eat chocolate, and hanging out with her husband.

Learn more about her at her website and sign up for her newsletter at http://heathertullis.com/ or her Facebook fan page http://www.facebook.com/HeatherTullisBooks.

303

www.ingramcontent.com/pod-product-compliance
Lightning Source LLC
Chambersburg PA
CBHW020944260626
47169CB00006B/1805